Nights with Grace

Rosie Scott was born in Wellington in 1948. After completing degrees in English and Drama, she travelled and worked at various occupations – including social work in New Zealand and Melbourne, publishing and newspaper work in London and Sydney and waitressing in Noumea. Her first book *Flesh and Blood*, a collection of poems, was followed by a stage play *Say Thank you to the Lady* which won the *Sunday Times* Bruce Mason Award. Her best-selling novel *Glory Days* was shortlisted for the National Book Award and was subsequently published in America and England. She has also published *Queen of Love*, a collection of stories. Rosie Scott is now a fulltime writer in Brisbane where she lives with her husband and two teenage daughters.

Also by Rosie Scott

Flesh and Blood (poetry)
Say Thank you to the Lady (stage play)
Glory Days
Queen of Love

Nights
with
Grace

Rosie Scott

MINERVA
AUSTRALIA

Published 1991 by Minerva Australia
an imprint of Mandarin
a division of the Octopus Publishing Group
22 Salmon Street, Port Melbourne, Victoria 3207

First published in Australia 1990 by William Heinemann
Australia

Printed and bound in Australia by Australian Print Group,

National Library of Australia
  cataloguing-in-publication data:

Scott, Rosie, 1948 –
  Nights with Grace.
  ISBN 1 86330 086 4.
  I. Title.

A823.3

To Dick, Elsie and Renée

GLOSSARY

Ara Tapu   sacred way or road

eis   garlands of flowers

Enewetak Atoll   an atoll in the Marshall Islands. The rats were
   found on the radioactive isle of Runit in Enewetak.

ivi o aku tupuna   the bones of our ancestors

kona   drunk

mamaruau   grandmother

papa'a   European

riri   crazy

taramea   starfish (slang for prostitute)

taro   edible root

ta te tangata e ruru ra, tana rai ia e kikoti   what a man sows
   he reaps

tupuna   ancestors

uramura   a sedate Cook Islands dance

ONE

The summer she turned seventeen, Grace spent a lot of her time dreaming. She sat for hours on the shadowy verandah fanning herself, gazing absently out at the garden where the trees flamed and glittered in the heat. Sitting there in the shade she could hear the walls of the house cracking as they dried out, and the weathered ironwood had the resinous, slightly acrid smell she had associated since childhood with hot langorous days dreaming on the sofa, the faint stirring of some indefinable longing.

She had lived there with her mother for years, the mynahs squawking outside in the trees and Te Rua Manga in the distance like a magic mountain rearing up above the jungle. There was something beautiful and momentous about the place — the wild clearing, the graceful, derelict house had an ease and unconstraint about them which always touched her imagination. It was a setting beyond the bounds of ordinary life, and to her the green peaks of the mountain on the horizon, the tangled garden were nostalgic images of freedom and possibility. She liked the sombre peace of the sky there, the heat and silence of the valley, the fact that the house was still as it had been since they'd found it. It was her favourite place for dreaming and that summer she sat there day after day, trancelike, as if she were travelling slowly through landscapes so compelling she had to give all her attention to them.

'So what are you going to do with your life?' her mother Mara asked in the middle of the summer.

It was one of those sweltering sweaty afternoons and the kitchen was swarming with flies. She was sitting drinking at the table, beautiful, her hair twisted carelessly in a knot at the back of her head, violet shadows under her eyes from a lifetime of sleepless nights.

'I might have mentioned this before Grace, but you're so creamy and thuggish at the moment I feel as if I ought to watch you for my own safety. For years if necessary.'

There was a man there of course, Raoul the Frenchman. He said apologetically,

'Mara, I don't believe it's necessary to talk like that to a teenage daughter. She is only growing into a beautiful woman, that's all. There is no mystery about this.'

'Ah yes,' she said, giving him a considering look with her tired, tired eyes. 'But a change like that is not as simple as it sounds. Some of them have to feed on their mother's flesh to get exactly the right texture to the skin.'

Raoul closed his eyes in pain, shaking his head slowly.

'Ah Mara. Tch, tch, tch,' was all he could say, darting a look at Grace as if afraid at what he'd see.

'I am actually here,' Grace said.

'If that were truly so, Grace,' her mother said. She glanced at Raoul's sorrowful face. 'It's all very well for you, Raoul. You don't actually have to live with her. Look at her there, so innocent it could melt your stony heart. She has all sorts of secrets she doesn't want to share with me now.'

'But Mara,' he said doggedly, 'that's no way to talk to your daughter. You'll never make me believe this, that talk like that is good for her.'

'It's a pathology to do with living in the jungle,' Grace said. 'Isolation, treachery, you name it. She has this dangerous gift with words and no outside influences.'

Raoul got up to find another drink. He was nervous about the wild talk going on around him. Balding, anxious, sweating, he was a civilised man who only wanted a little kindness.

'So you are enjoying your job?' he said, his voice scratchy with trying to please.

'Yes she is,' Mara said after a short silence. 'She loves it, don't you Grace?' She began to sing in her lovely booze-cracked voice, *'Oh Paradiso! Oh come to me! The sleep of death brings you always closer!'*

'What do you mean, brings you always closer?' Grace asked. She was extremely tired. 'It sounds all wrong.'

She was making inroads into life even if her mother hadn't noticed. Her dreaminess only camouflaged intense mental processes. Her allegiances were to a private self that she never revealed to anyone, to the place where she was born, and to certain people in her life.

Sometimes late at night she looked at herself secretly in the mirror, watched her eyes and skin so closely that each feature lost context and became a map of unknown territories. Gaping pores, the cataclysmic beginnings of a pimple on the corner of her mouth, her eyes liquid and shining with the light of consciousness, riding like quicksilver in their sockets. Saliva bubbling on the roots of her tongue, hairs sprouting like straw on her cheeks, her teeth close up a dirty yellow. The ugliness gave her something definite, it made her able to see her own physical particularity. Lying on the mattress, she felt her breasts, slipped one hand tenderly between her soft thighs and touched the rough hair, the wetness inside. It gave her a powerful feeling of understanding, as if she had known all along about the mysterious processes going on in her, spreading like bubbles through her blood. At times like that she was preoccupied with monitoring herself, listening for signs, she heard voices, her blood singing in her veins, the quiet formation of intricate tender structures going on inside her. She looked at her face in the mirror, her eyes gravely staring back at her and felt the power of her own existence stirring.

She said to herself, testing, 'An old woman at seventeen,' because she wanted to see her own answering amused smile, feel the comfort of her existence, the perfect understanding between her and her mirror self.

It was the same with her daily life, her job at the Paradise Bar, her long walk home each night along the Ara Tapu, with the rustling jungle around her and the sound of sea as regular and familiar to her as her own heartbeat. She felt all the silent awareness of an animal as it stands alert for danger, dissolving itself into the leaves if need be.

Because that was her life, the jungle round the house, the night walk through lonely roads, a huge black fish swimming silently underneath her rasping her back as she floated in the dark, men calling to her hungrily, the long vigils in private places.

And there was also her mother and the legend of her. The mother who arrived in Rarotonga years ago, stepping off the boat with her husband, was so beautiful that the entire wharf came to a standstill. Her husband, a Land Court judge, was newly appointed but there was no interest in him that morning. Everyone had eyes only for her, his young wife, that stunning languid beauty on his arm. With those startling blue eyes like reflections of the sea, hair down to her waist, dreamy, preoccupied with her own secret thoughts, she was like a vision to their sleeping town.

Grace had always been able to see her vividly, that golden girl, as she stepped off the wharf into the crowd of waiting admirers, like a princess going to the scaffold. Again and again in slow motion she imagined her until the scene dissolved into the pure wash of the Pacific air. A halo of gold for her hair, china-pink for her cheeks and dress, blood-red for the ring on her finger. Grace still saw everything as simply and clearly as she did when she was first told the story as a child. But she had soon realised that not many daughters had childhood legends of such richness and cruelty to feed them, and also disentangle themselves from.

'It's not as if I haven't tried,' Mara told her once when she was too small to understand. 'It's not my fault if circumstances were against me. I've always done my best, Grace. I can't help it if the Lord's given me such an unruly sex drive.'

She had burst out laughing at the time, and Grace joined in out of love. It was just after they had been thrown out of their rented house. The landlord had found Mara in bed with the Congregational minister. Someone had told them about a house abandoned in the jungle, so they moved in that day and had been camping there ever since. They slept on mattresses, there were some Island mats scattered around, Mara's books, a cooker, the TV for Mara's videos, a feeling of dusty peace in the rooms. That was their life together. Mara occasionally went up to the shop looking like a decrepit duchess, her dress dirty round the hem and covered with strange maplike stains, everyone calling her a whore and a drunk behind her back. Not that she cared, because she never judged herself by other people's standards. Her life had been a tour through the underside of the polite society of their town for years, so she had no illusions. Being fawned over and ridiculed was all the same to Mara, nothing ever stopped the secret pilgrimage of men to her bedroom window. With her crazy sardonic courage and her arrogance there was nothing she was scared of.

It wasn't the same with Grace, she knew she had none of that kind of life-burning charisma, none of the wicked qualities which would make people change their lives and follow, dazzled down her path as they did with Mara. She was too quiet to attract that sort of attention. Her mother was no help to her because she had her own daily, lifetime predicaments to handle, with little energy left over for anyone else.

'Now listen, Grace. I have to be honest, I don't know who your father is. There were so many of them around at the time. It's shitty for you Grace, I know, but all I can do is narrow it down. And that's a dangerous exercise,' she told her.

An unknown father wasn't news to Grace but it still wounded her. When she came home from work and sat alone in her bedroom, the heavy scent of frangipani wafting through the open window, she wrote poems to her lost father, a big glittering piece of writing spreading like a sheet of ice. On the other side of the house, the cold blue light of the video flickered on her mother's unconscious face, her snores rocked the foundations. On these late sweet nights Mara slept the deep sleep of the righteous, her snores echoing like the roar of a lion. It was a sound as comforting to Grace as the sea.

TWO

That summer there was an invasion of butterflies because of the unusual heat. Clouds of them settled in the trees, moving their wings in unison as if they were breathing together in some mysterious collusion. At the water gardens where Grace and Mara had come that afternoon, they were so numerous that gazing up into the leaves at them made Grace dizzy. She felt stretched thin enough to be drawn like vapour towards them into that desirable sea-green world where they floated dreamily. They were like spirits flickering in the leaves, ghosts of the extinct birds an old man had once told Grace about. He had imitated their calls for her and lovingly described their plumage by showing her the pearly inside of a shell and a poinciana flower; and she never forgot it.

She often thought about the birds when she was in the gardens because the presence of the past was so strong there. Families came silently up through the paths to work the taro, they stood knee-deep in the water, and after their work sat gossiping in the shade as their ancestors had done for generations.

It was as if the past had been collected there like water in a deep pool. The people who had coaxed the shimmering system down the hills all those centuries ago, their descendants who had been coming ever since to plant taro, the birds that once flew in dazzling flocks through the jungle still lingered in its depths, emerging to the surface every now and then as fleetingly as cloud reflections on the water.

'You remind me of a Southern belle. All pale and melted in the heat. Complicated internally. Waiting for the beau who never comes,' Mara said trying to be friendly. She had come up with her for a picnic, an increasingly rare occasion, and was sitting by the pool with her feet in the water. She was wearing a straw hat with stained pink cloth roses. Grace, half-dozing on the soft grass, struggled into a sitting position at the sound of her mother's voice. She was flushed and sweating, the heat had become more intense while she had been dreaming there. As she sat up groggily people went past them down the track towards Avarua, a brown-haired man with an exuberant face who stared at her so hard he brushed into the ferns at the edge of the track. The woman behind him with velvet legs and a mass of curls said something laughing to him and hit at him with a stick she was carrying. They went on down the path, she could hear the soft thud of their feet and their laughter.

'What's the time?' she asked, thinking about the man and woman. The girl's body and hair were so magazine perfect, she glanced down at her own broad white thighs sadly.

'I don't know.'

'You're like a vampire, Mara,' she said, drawing her legs up under her skirt far too late. 'You sit out in the sun there and you don't even look hot. Your skin always stays cold.'

'I know. It's probably the sherry, preserving my cells.'

She was looking intently down into the depths of the taro pool, her sunglasses reflecting the shiver of the water.

'You should see the mosquito larvae here. Little wriggling shadows. They're like sperm. No wonder this place is such a killer. Is there anything more to eat?'

Grace looked, but there were only some hot, bruised-looking mangoes all jumbled up in the dirty lining of the bag.

'We have ridiculous picnics,' Mara said, standing up and shaking out her dress. 'When I was a girl we had cool things in ice, green salads, chicken, champagne. Sitting on gracious lawns with admirers very much in evidence. I would have liked that for you.'

'Really,' said Grace, gazing lovingly at the butterflies. 'I can't believe that.'

'Of course. But here I am, with a half-wild thing, her skin creased like a baby's, who hardly says a word. I've reared a little changeling I think sometimes.'

'Wild child,' sang Grace, thinking of a song she'd heard recently on the radio.

'You should have got up earlier. We'll be late for Raoul.'

'Raoul?'

'I've arranged for him to meet us at the beginning of the track. In his taxi.'

'Porora told me it was dangerous to sleep under a teitei tree,' Grace said, picking up the rubbish, yawning and stretching as she went.

'Why?'

'They're sacred. The legend is that the roots come through the earth and strangle you.'

'Oh dear, Grace. You sound like a folklore series on the back of some sort of cereal packet. Did you know that the Hopi Indians believe the earth will die if they do not make sacrifice at full moon? With all the colours out of register. It's terribly sad that the lack of intellectual stimulation here has made you prey to such glibness. Hollywood trash mysticism at its worst.'

'Oh don't be so silly. It's a manner of speaking. It's just a metaphor.'

They started the trek down, trailing their basket in the heat, sitting under the trees for periods of rest so they were nearly an hour late when they finally reached the end of the track. Raoul just smiled at them both with his tinsey little French mouth and helped them into the baking car. The plastic seat cover was so hot it burnt the skin at the back of her legs.

'That's OK,' he said, even though no one had apologised. 'I can wait all day for two such beautiful women.'

He even had a hibiscus each for them. Mara put hers in her hair, she seemed happy for some reason even though she had complained all the way down about the sadness of their picnics.

Grace said, 'Can you drop me off at work first?'

'What do you think, Madam? Shall I take you home last?' he said, his doggy eyes in the mirror meeting Mara's in the age-old unspoken agreement. Grace almost envied her for once, a languid afternoon in bed with an adoring man, even if it was only Raoul with his anxious eyes, sweating mat of black hair on his chest.

'Yes — to the house of the witches as they all so charmingly call it.'

'But they are not talking about you,' Raoul said, quick to defend Mara as always. 'Pardon me. When the Sutcliffes walk out it was the kids who call it the witches' house after they break the windows and make pipi in the bath.'

'I know. I was only joking. But we haven't exactly altered the ambience, have we, Gracie?'

There was so much truth in this that they all remained silent. Grace thought of the bareness of the rooms, the calm old design of the house with fondness.

'I've often wondered about them. Leaving the house to moulder away like that. They've never come back to claim it or anything,' she said, mostly to herself.

'They went silly,' Raoul said, doing a screeching U-turn to pull up beside the Paradise. 'Troppo. They had no other thought in their heads than to escape. So. There it is. Your place of work, the Paradiso! For an angel.'

'See you later,' she said to her mother. She had the distinct feeling that the previous owners of their house were more forlorn than wildly insane. She had always seen them clearly, he a kind-faced man, she fretful, both of them dwarfed by the jungle as they chipped away at their merciless garden. It wouldn't have been the first time she'd seen white people in Rarotonga defeated by the unseen forces they had never taken into consideration. But then Raoul knew his gossip, he was the aficionado among experts and the facts he unearthed always had a kind of truth about them.

There were only three customers at the bar, friends of Joe's, and a solitary tourist reading his paper at the table, an empty cup in front of him. The radio was playing forties music softly to itself from the shelf above the old silver till. Joe was at the bar serving in his shirt-sleeves. As usual he was half-drunk.

'Where you been, Totty?' he asked. 'We almost gave up on you.'

'We went up the Takuvaine valley. Mara's annual outing. Am I late?' Grace sat down at the bar and nodded hello at the customers. Joe poured her out a beer. His hands were very shaky.

'Yeah. Could be. Could be. Me watch stopped. Takuvaine, eh? The water gardens? Never been there. I heard it was black with mozzies.'

'You should go,' Grace remarked, without really believing it.

'Me? I can't be bothered to go to Avarua these days,' he said, wiping the bar fussily. 'Too many tourists.'

'But Joe, that's only five minutes up the blooming road.'

'Now listen, Gracie girl, I can do what I like at my age without having some young trollop taking the mickey out of me.'

'Go on,' she said drinking greedily, thirsty from her long walk in the sun. 'You're not old.'

'I wouldn't tell you me age even if you went on your bended knees,' he said, winking at the old men. 'Which you wouldn't in a month of Sundays. And that's a bloody fact as well.'

They smiled obediently into their beer. They had the swollen dazed look of hardened beer drinkers, they always looked to Joe for guidance. All his friends were from New Zealand, old men who talked in a desultory way about racing and the weather or just simply sat staring ahead, holding their glass of beer in front of them like a shield.

'I know anyway, Joe,' Grace said, wiping her mouth with the back of her hand. 'And I'm shocked.'

'Now listen, Grace,' he said, leaning over to whisper wetly in her ear. 'She's on the warpath. I want to duck out the back for a minute, so can you take over? Not let on like. Just take over in a relaxed sort of way?'

'Are you going to play cards or what?'

'God's truth, Gracie. Not a hope. On my mother's grave. I wouldn't even think about it.'

'Porora's upset. About the bones under the motel. That's all.'

'I know. You don't have to tell me, Totty. I've seen it in her eyes.' He made a grotesque grimace and popped his false teeth out, crossing his wicked old eyes.

'Don't do it, Joe.'

'Bossing is it now,' he said, lifting up the bar flap and dodging out with the quickness of a boy. 'Since when has the Rose of Tralee taken to bossing?'

'You promised.'

'All right then. Be a good girl and look after the shop. Your uncle Joe will be back before you can say Jack Robinson.'

'Don't upset her. I mean it.'

She was thinking of the man she'd seen at the water gardens. He was like a faun with that mocking face, slightly swollen eyes, the curls blowing like thistledown round his head. She sighed, stretched, smoked a cigarette. She felt lazy, langorous. The motionless men sat at the bar each in their silent aura, as the shadows fell around them and the radio blatted softly like the murmuring of people in another room. A very faint breeze stirred the strips of plastic hanging at the door.

The swing music on the radio reminded her of her mother's past, the stories of loss and nostalgia she had been told all her life. It was as if they were her own personal memories, so clearly could she imagine that era. Conversations about the war, the aroma of roast dinners, velvet lawns, picnics by the river and singalongs in the evening. Young men fawning over the docile women who sat sewing and smiling by the fire. Her beautiful mother, like a flame, playing the grand piano, dancing with the Prime Minister, learning four languages and then falling from grace with such flamboyance that all of it went spinning off into the distance forever.

For that moment, listening to the sweet tinny orchestra was like being inside her mother's mind, living her life. With her mother's eyes she could see their house, their life together as something wild and forlorn, without meaning. In the bare high-ceilinged rooms where the video flickered day and night and the greenish jungle light poured through their windows like the sea, there would never be anything to remind her of home. Grace thought of her mother sitting out her days there, patient as a witch, watching videos and drinking, the great jungle insects crawling slowly up the walls.

'Coming,' she said, though no one had called her.

THREE

Grace crossed the road to sit and rest for a while under the shade of the poinciana on the corner. She was walking to work, and the morning people, trees, flowers, cars glowed and hummed warmly, their colours streaming into her eyes so strongly that she winced away from them. Going down the road was like passing through a carefully drawn child's painting, with its scarlet hibiscus flowers on the roadside verges, houses tucked away under swathes of green like dollhouses, the graves of ancestors lovingly tended in the front gardens. Along the paths lines of kaitava were planted in neat rows, the leaves were freshly striped as if someone had got up very early in the morning and painted them on. Washing hung on the bushes, people waved and laughed as they rode past in battered cars, Toyota trucks, bikes, on their ceaseless circuit of the island. Beneath the roar of traffic and construction sites there was the steady soft heartbeat of the sea.

A man on a bike rode so closely past her that she felt him brushing her side and heard his breath rasping in his chest. She just had time to step back, glimpse a working back, slippery with sweat, hair clustered damply, a man glowing with heat and relentless movements before he raced on ahead. He turned back to look at her as she stood there, surprised, slightly angry. In that second of turning before he had to give full attention back to righting the swing of the bike he gave her a smile of great tenderness as if he recognised her. She saw then that he was the man she'd noticed at Takuvaine.

She watched him go as he rode away under the trees, light streaming off him like water. She imagined his long-legged girlfriend at the hotel waking and stretching, sighing when she heard the sound of his clothes dropping to the floor. There was something dazzling about him, his energy, just a glimpse of him touched off her own delight in the world, that most secret exultant part of her which smiled so tenderly and understandingly at herself in the mirror. He was like someone she already knew. She gazed without seeing at the familiar one-roomed shop smothered in bougainvillaea, its faded Choysa tea sign, the chooks scratching in the dust in the doorway. The thought of him was as compelling as a burst of fireworks exploding miles up in the sky, she felt the same quick lift of the heart, as she stared after him.

When she finally arrived at work, Porora was banging glasses down on the bar and did not look up at her. Grace was used to seeing Porora brooding and she didn't feel like commenting. She put on her apron and picked up the straw broom with ostentatious purpose. The bar where she worked was down in the rubble of the breakwater, it was only a shack with a few torn palms in pots by the door, a faded awning which flapped in the sea wind. She kept meaning to clean it up in front, but even the sea looked tattered and old down there, it bobbed with plastic and bottles from the industrial part of Avarua washing up tiredly on the cold, dirty stones of the artificial breakwater.

Inside it was shadowy and smelt of tropical damp and beer, as the windows and doors were usually kept shut against the wind.

'You say nothing. You always late. I come in here and clean up this place.'

Porora towered like an ugly warrior queen in the shadows of the bar. The smooth black coils of hair sleeked back from her face were as soft and shining as plumage, the scarlet pareu she was wearing glimmered royally. She flicked the towel at Grace, the glass she was holding minuscule inside her swollen brown hand.

'Sorry,' Grace said.

'Aaargh,' Porora said flopping down beside the bar, her hands over her eyes, flesh spilling over the sides of the slim stool.

'A cup of coffee? A little marsala?' Grace asked, settling thankfully into her daily routine, the tiny tarnished stage of her workplace, cosily insulated from the world.

'You know what they done now?' Porora crooned, her eyes tight shut. 'You know how they dug them up out in the light of day, scattered them like chicken bones? Well, yesterday the *papa'a* poured concrete on them. So they are gone forever under that building, that motel of theirs.' She gulped down the glass of marsala Grace handed silently to her.

'I don't believe it. Why didn't you tell that minister?'

'Gone forever under that motel,' she repeated her eyes still closed. 'That minister he good for creeping up on a few peoples, jumping on some wives. OK?'

'Who? Mr Nathan?'

'That's him, Grace. No good, he say. The *papa'a* boss say this is the custom in New Zealand, those bones are too old for respect.'

Grace drank her own coffee, shaken. She had gone to the place the day before when Porora had first told her about it. She had noticed the child's skull lying by the tree first, earth clinging to its eye sockets, before she saw the rest of them — bones everywhere, scattered among the rocks and ploughed-up earth where the bulldozer had been. She had stood very still in shock, listening to the sound of the sea, the cicadas clicking, in a place suddenly grown evil.

'What can we do?' she asked Porora, taking a small swig of marsala herself. 'Eh, Porora?'

'What exactly you want to do? Dig through the concrete? The *papa'a* got no respect, that's their big trouble.'

'Only some *papa'a*,' Grace said, but Porora heard nothing. She went and stood by the grimy window at the back of the bar, her arms folded, staring out. She looked baffled and malevolent, there was enough to worry about without *papa'a* trouble. Looking after the bar all her life in the killing tropical damp, the smell of booze ingrained in her skin, Joe to restrain, were all too much for an old woman as it was. Then she had grandchildren to teach, social obligations, all sorts of other mysterious commitments which Grace didn't even enquire about.

'No respect at all,' she said. There was the first customer of the day to serve, the bar to clean. She left her coffee cup to cool on the bar as she moved around slowly, cranking up the routine of a lifetime. When Grace was a small girl, she used to try to imitate the way Porora moved her hands, how she touched every object tenderly as if it were very frail, her hands always graceful.

'You look particularly dreamy this morning,' Porora said, irritated with her, as she stood motionless, broom in hand, thinking.

'Maybe she's in love. You got a boyfriend yet, Grace?' the old man asked familiarly. He covered his drink lovingly with shaky hands, a roll-your-own hanging from his lips. Porora went out the back and they heard the wet thud of her machete as she started to cut up the pineapples.

'Yes,' said Grace. 'In my dreams.' She was used to heading off men and their embarrassingly open fantasies about her. She never had much small talk with the customers, but Porora didn't seem to mind. Usually the local drunks left her alone; nicotine-stained, nerveless with the booze, they were too far gone to give her a hard time. She was surprised at Jock's comment. It was only the tourists who bothered her. Occasionally they found their way down to the Paradise from the big hotels; instantly recognisable by the t-shirts with crude messages on them. They were usually men with big strong legs, the soft skin of people used to power and comfort. She could almost hear their brains grinding into gear every time one of them came in. They watched her for a while, incredulous, electric with assumptions, eyeing her greedily as if they had just stumbled on a treasure and were looking around slyly before claiming it as their rightful. It was always unbearable, the heat they gave off as they manoeuvred for position and made their conversation. They talked to her as if they were the centre of the wild Western world, as if she only had to give the word and they'd be there, guiding her through its mazy wicked wonderland.

She was used to superficial relationships with men, but it still made her uneasy, frightened of the power they could have. Since she was a child, there had always been a heady current in the air that she had had to defend herself from, her mother's voluptuous slide into temporary submission, men hanging around, sex in the air, the desperate sounds from the bedroom. Even when she was very young it was something she desired and feared, ugly men's bodies, peering up at their solid hairy legs, seeing those special grins sliding off and on their faces like jam. In those early years Mara's boyfriends were usually the respectable men who ran things. Grace used to see their pictures in the local paper, they were giving out trophies, smiling kindly as they bent over the lucky recipient. She had already seen them with their pants down, their faces gaping and flushing, wicked natures in full flight. Even now she was seventeen, her mental picture of men had not changed much; hairy, shuffling, smiling in sly anticipation, they waited in the dark shabby houses of her childhood for pleasures she could not even guess at.

'Jock, he's going *riri*,' Porora grumbled. She had a pile of pineapples neatly sliced on a plate for Grace to cover with white sugar. 'He too old for love.'

Porora never complained to the customers directly but so strong was her unspoken contempt that people were invariably flustered by the diffused malevolence in the air. They always smiled a lot when they came in, hoping to please her.

'The boys they stop work for two days. On the site,' she said, settling at the bar for a minute, pouring herself another marsala.

'About the bones?'

'The boss he say cut it out or I'll get more *papa'a* from New Zealand in. Lose your jobs, you black boys.'

Grace slid the pineapple slices onto each dish, the sweetish rich smell filling the air, attracting clouds of flies. It was one of the smells of the Paradise and she inhaled it greedily.

'Oh yes,' she said, dreading what would come next.

'And then he make them pour concrete over,' Porora said, tears on her cheeks. 'All the dead.'

'Please don't be sad,' Grace said desperately. Her life with her mother had not prepared her for showing affection, but all the same she put her arms awkwardly around Porora's shoulders.

'Ah well,' Porora said, brushing away the tears and Grace's arm after allowing herself a second of relaxation against her, 'God will provide. I have the comfort of the good Lord to provide for me and my children.'

That night Grace went for her first swim in weeks. The sea was like black silk against her skin as she lay on her back floating silently, staring up at the stars. All she had to do was splash her arms and legs gently now and then to stay afloat, readjust her spine to the wash of the sea, close her eyes when a wavelet rippled over her face. She even sang a couple of songs to herself as she watched her white limbs flash like fish in and out of the dark water. 'You are my sunshine,' she sang, letting the water wash over her until she was half-drowned in its sweetness.

FOUR

On Saturday nights the seedy atmosphere of the listless afternoons at the Paradise was transformed magically into carnival, a private intense celebration for the people of the neighbourhood. Grace always liked watching the changes in people as booze and desire, the party spirit took hold. Churchgoing expressions, accommodating smiles meant for tourists and customers gave way to ease and inwardness, people became as surly, thoughtful or joyous as they wanted to be. It was the night and the place for letting go the hypocrisies of island life.

The women looked like queens with their pareus and the rich flowers in their hair, they formed lines to dance by themselves dreamily, their hands weaving soft signals in the air, eyes half-closed in ecstasy. The men stood sturdily at the back of the bar, heads thrown back, faces distorted with the anguish and joy of their fierce singing. Grace watched them, absorbed, their taut throat muscles, the shine of sweat on their skin; they sang the silvery and passionately sweet Rarotongan songs as achingly as a South American compañero. There was the same yearning note of controlled intensity and tenderness. The vibration of dancing feet on the wooden floor, the sound of guitars, the roar of drinking men remained only a background to the singing as it rose, radiant with desire above the din. That night someone had opened up all the doors and windows because of the heat, and the place was alive with the roaring of the sea. Traffic coming past from Avarua, the smells of petrol, frangipani, dust from the road poured in to clash with the distinctively Paradise smells of sweat and mustiness.

As Grace worked alone at the bar, she caught occasional glimpses of Porora through the seethe of bodies and shadows, doing the *uramura*, her face impassive as she was respectfully applauded. She reminded Grace of one of those wooden Russian dolls whenever she danced, her bulk graceful and bell-shaped, tucked in a comely way round the edges, her insides full of secrets and surprises.

She had just got up from the floor after spiking a new cask of beer, when she glanced up and saw the man from the water gardens standing in front of the bar, staring at her. Every part of her body suddenly became alive to him, it was as if there was a trailing vapour between them ready to catch fire. She stared at him in panic.

'Hello.'

'Hello.' She moved to lean against the bar for help, her heart was beating so painfully.

'You work here?' he asked. It was almost impossible for her to meet his eyes or see that tender mouth of his so close.

'Yes.'

'Beer please. Two thanks.'

She noticed that his forearms were perfect, the shirt sleeves rolled up to show graceful arms, soft dark hair, competent hands resting lightly on the counter in front of him. His body was relaxed towards her, and she was flustered by his closeness. He gave her the money, she poured the beers and handed them to him. He hesitated slightly as if to say something else and she turned away, too quickly, to serve someone else. The second beer was probably for his girlfriend she thought, trying to recover. At the same time she looked back as if she had all the time in the world to give him her most private smile, but he had disappeared, melted into the crowd.

She stood looking after him, bereft, wondering why she had rejected a man so beautiful, when all around her, as an object lesson, drunken people wept and drank and sang their hearts out, sensuality and triumphant singing filling the air with richness and danger. There was something missing in her she thought, suddenly anguished. Her upbringing and her looks had cut her off from ease with people, she was so used to looking past an admiring man that she had had no practice in letting anyone see her secret side, the mirror Grace, the real person. There was an automatic withdrawal whenever she felt the nagging current of peoples' wants pushing and tugging at her. She had insulted him, a gentle man, just for that. Her mother called it her Princess Anne syndrome, which of course was an insult because Mara despised royalty. Lighten up for Christ's sake she'd say, drawing on her cigarette. Have a good time.

Grace smiled slightly at the thought and went on serving mechanically, head down, unable to speak. She decided that if he came back it was a signal to her, and she would be able to tell him everything, open up to him like a flower and never let it happen again, a magic chance. She waited all night but it was only Joe who came, shouldering his way through the bar, shaking hands with his customers, slapping backs and missing, slurring his words like a movie drunk.

'Ah you little soldier,' he said. 'Not a bloody soul to help you either.'

'It's all right.'

'Where's me wife?'

'She was dancing.'

He looked at her closely. 'You upset with me then, Gracie?' he asked. 'Not that I blame you. Listen to me, Totty, the whole day off, full pay tomorrow.'

'Thanks, Joe,' she said hardly listening to him.

'Ha ha!' he bawled so loudly people turned to look. 'That fooled you! April fool! Duffer!' The strings of saliva in his mouth glistened and vibrated as his slack old mouth opened wide. 'It's Sunday tomorrow!'

'Ah, you ain't funny, Joe.'

'What's the matter then? Eh? You look downcast and sad, my girl. Downcast and sad. Oh Rose of Tralee,' he sang. 'Two beers is it? Good on you, here they are, wet and bubbling as you'd wish. What's the trouble, my darlin'?'

'Nothing.'

He looked blankly at her and then burst into one of his silent, drunken laughs. 'Nothing? You can't fool your old uncle Joe. Look at that face.'

He lurched against the bar, knocking over glasses, his face stupid with booze. 'Sunday, Sunday,' he sang in a Mamas and Papas falsetto, his eyes sliding around dangerously.

Grace watched the blur of celebration in front of her, hands reaching for the beer she poured, the sweaty dancers smiling at her for the transaction, making little comments to her out of their good nature. Her dress was drenched with sweat and splashes of beer, she moved slowly, her heart aching with depression.

'So where is she? Where's me wife?' Joe bawled in her ear, his face distorted with rage. Grace almost jumped out of her skin with shock. It was the sign that he had reached the final stage of drunkenness. It always came on suddenly and fiercely and it was always jealous fears about Porora.

'She gone home with Nooangatau. They in bed now!' called someone. Everyone knew about Joe, it was part of the night's entertainment. Grace caught hold of his skinny, wet, juddering arm.

'She's home in bed probably, Joe. Asleep.'

'Thassright Joe. The Duchess knows!' It was past midnight and the crowd was tiring slightly. People pressed forward eager to see the familiar drama.

'Where's my fucking wife?' he called, despairing, lifting up his old muzzle like a wolf, saliva frothing his chin.

'Gone to bed,' said Grace again.

'You're only shielding her, Gracie darlin'. Shielding her!' His voice rose to a shriek. He began to laugh silently to himself again, working himself up for another scream. Porora's eldest son, Pupuke who was sitting in the corner by himself, singing Elvis songs to his own accompaniment, put his guitar down gently with a resigned sigh. He came over and picked up his stepfather in his fat arms as if he were a baby. Joe lay there sucking his mouth in reflectively, his legs dangling like sticks. All the fight seemed to have gone out of him.

'Where shall I put this old man?' Pupuke asked rhetorically. He was a courteous person, but he no longer bothered to hide his impatience. He came through the back, carrying Joe gently with Grace following and laid him down on the mattress kept for that purpose in the wash-house out the back. Grace usually left him to sleep it off at the Paradise. Porora suffered enough from her bad dreams without having Joe in her bed. In the last stage of drunkenness he was like a goblin baby, his little face hideously contorted, he wet the sheets two or three times at least in the night. The mattress in the wash-house was stained and evil-smelling, but Grace hauled it out on hot days to dry and air, and covered it decently with a blanket during the day for Porora's sake.

'He's a bloody terror, that man,' Pupuke said with a smile, shaking his head. 'You can manage this boy OK?' He walked back to his guitar, every step shaking the place, his tight teal-blue pants magnificently sheathing his gargantuan bum.

'*Love me tender, love me true,*' he sang, his moon face dotingly bent over the guitar.

Grace always stayed to lock up after everyone had gone, in a silence that descended like a wall. The place dwindled and blurred when it was empty, it was like a deserted movie set, the air humming from old dramas. The walls of the bar added to the artificiality of the atmosphere, they were like a shrine with mysterious objects glimmering in corners and alcoves. There were shell necklaces hung in loops over the framed photographs, plaster half-vases with plastic flowers, a painted silhouette of hula girls and palm trees, a huge Hollywood moon. Everything was greyish with dust. Grace had long since given up trying to clean them, she barely even noticed them any more except sometimes at the end of a long night when she was too weary to move and her eyes rested on them for reassurance.

That night she had swept up the worst of the night's debris and checked on Joe who lay as still as an old doll on his narrow mattress. She sat for a while at the table, out of habit, her feet up, mind blank, a can of beer in front of her, looking out the open doors into the night.

It was quiet outside now except for an unseen group of people talking in soft voices on the beach below. It was a soothing Pacific night, heavy, fragrant, alive with tenderness — it made her ache with longing. She felt so lethargic she did not want to find the motivation to get up, close the doors and walk home ever again. It was like being woken up in the middle of the night with some terrible unnameable grief. She thought of Raoul and Mara bickering and drinking at home and wished suddenly that she could just go to sleep in the bar. As she sat there debating with herself tiredly, she heard a sound outside, like an empty beer can clinking against the ground.

'Who's that?' she called and her tiredness miraculously vanished when she saw him. He was waiting for her in the dark, hunched onto the rickety log seat by the palm tree, his legs balanced wide apart against the thin plank. He gazed at the sky, absorbed, lost in thought, momentarily peaceful, his body as desirable and familiar to her as if she had known him all her life. There were two empty cans beside him where he had been waiting.

'Hello, Grace,' he said, seeing her and standing up awkwardly.

'Hello.'

'I wanted to wait for you,' he said nervously. 'There didn't seem to be another way to do it.'

There was a silence. She could just make him out as her eyes became accustomed to the darkness. He was leaning against the wall looking at her. She saw he was wearing jeans, a white shirt undone at the throat, sleeves rolled loosely, white espadrilles. He had become electric, his body charged up, he was glimmering with tension as he stood facing her.

'I hope I'm not being offensive or anything. I can't help it.'

Grace thought of the usual way men talked to her at the bar and smiled at him. She felt dizzy with relief to see him in front of her, she wanted to kiss him in gratitude. It was another chance after all, and she felt her defences melt away in his smiling presence.

'Can I walk you home then?' he asked politely, his eyes on her.

'Yes,' she said so softly he had to bend his beautiful head to catch her words. She started to walk and he came beside her. Grace had never seen a man of such beauty before, but there he was, breathing easily beside her, the faint scratchy sound of his jeans rasping as he picked his way up the rocky path to the road.

'You're very quiet,' he said in his warm voice.

She said, 'Yes, quiet, but very deep.' She glanced at him sideways and saw him smiling down at the road as if he recognised something valuable. Her own answering smile to herself was like her mirror smile, a sign of absolute complicity. The walk seemed to go on forever as they moved quietly, not touching or speaking. She concentrated on listening to his breathing, the pump of his heart, catching glimpses of the serious shine of his profile. She was sharply aware of their exact location to each other and the world, in her mind's eye she saw the sea lapping on the beach below them, encircling the island and stretching for thousands of lonely miles into the darkness, and above them the stars swinging over their heads, fierce as frozen lightning. The two of them were like a small luminous spot in the middle of endless darkness, the night arching over them millions of light-years into the past.

'I keep seeing you,' he said. 'Not that it's an imposition or anything. Every time I see you you're in a dream. Head down, waddling like a duck.'

She looked over at him, confused. He said hastily, 'Oh, that's just a poem. I didn't mean you of course.'

'Did you like the water gardens?' She was being airily brave as the darkness gave her licence.

'The sleeping woman under the tree?' he said seriously. 'Yes I like that more than anything I've ever seen. Bar none.' He coughed and looked up at the sky. Grace felt her stomach lift as if there was a great bird in there beating its wings. She wanted to hug herself to keep the feeling hidden down inside her.

'I'm sorry, I'm finding it very hard to talk to you. Every time I see you I become ridiculous. I have no techniques for this, if you know what I mean.'

'I do. I know it exactly.'

It was as if they were flowing together into some deep delicious pool but the current was too fast. Each clumsy word drew them closer, it was only silence which saved them from drowning.

'This is my place,' she said. The cat came bounding up the track to meet her, then paused to observe the stranger, her triangular face disdainful.

'Is this yours?' he asked, picking her up. He stroked her gently, his face momentarily absorbed, his hands moving firmly down her quivering length and carefully caressing her little wet belly. She purred and squirmed and submitted. It reminded Grace of certain dreams of hers, the way his hands stroked so confidently.

'Can I see you again? Tomorrow?'

'Yes,' she said. 'Of course yes. Please.'

He kept stroking the cat, but raised his eyes to her face. 'Say please again,' he said, his hand not stopping.

'Please,' she said, 'please.' She leaned against a tree. She felt an ache start up again deep in her stomach.

'I can't believe this.' He put the cat down on the grass. They both watched her run away through the trees.

'Can't believe what?' she whispered.

'You know,' he said and came over to her. She could see his eyes and mouth shining in the dark. 'I feel like a teenager. I've been obsessed with you all week and now you're here in the flesh smiling at me and saying please. That's what I can't believe.'

'Seventeen I am,' Grace said. 'Seventeen and never been kissed.' She had become reckless with love. 'I'm warning you. I have a long sad history. Like the creature in Alice in Wonderland.'

'The Mock Turtle. I thought so. To look at you I would have thought so. This pale suffering beast with eyes like stars.'

'Another poem?'

'I don't know,' he said, his eyes closed. 'It just came to me. I honestly can't talk any more. Something happens when I touch your skin.'

She knew it was nearly time to stop talking and lie down with this man in that lovely drenched expectant silence before sex.

'Well, maybe a few kisses here and there,' was all she said before he took his shirt off and folded it on the ground for them to lie on, and the cat raced back down the path, crazy with the excitements of the night.

FIVE

'I dreamt about the bones under the motel,' Grace told Porora when they were cleaning up the Paradise the next day.

'Yes?' said Porora, stopping work to show her interest.

'I was on my own and I had Joe's pick — you know the one he uses to dig a hole for the rubbish. I was digging into the concrete with it, but all I could see were worms.'

'What kind of worms?'

'Long black ones.'

'Is that all? That's not much of a dream, my girl.'

They had all the windows and doors open, Porora was washing up glasses at the tiny cracked sink, while Grace with a scarf around her head was sweeping clouds of dust out into the courtyard. They were both sweating and drinking continuously from a large plastic jug Porora had filled with cordial and put there for easy reach.

'You are a good girl, coming in here to help to clean up with your old aunty like this. Dreaming your *papa'a* dreams.'

'I wish someone would do something,' Grace said. 'Instead of talking.'

'I think about those people buried there all the time. You got to remember we've had our ways mocked since the first day the *papa'a* came here. I talk to the old people.

They know there's been no respect for us. Those bones, they at the end of a long line snaking right back.'

'I know,' Grace said stubbornly, 'you've told me before.'

'Well learn, girl. Get it into your head. Those politicians we got, they *papa'a* with brown skins. Money, plane trips, big houses. See how the people leave, leave, leave. See the empty houses everywhere in the bush. But no one talks anything, we are all too polite. Smile, smile that's all we do. And so what about you? Standing staring at me while I work. What do you do besides talk?'

'I was just thinking about what you said.'

'Your mother came in here yesterday,' Porora said venomously.

'What for?'

'A drink. What do you think? She have one beer and then go. With her boyfriend. I don't think I ever seen that one here before.'

'You know Raoul,' Grace said, disbelieving. She was used to Porora's allegorical stories.

'A fine woman like that. Not many in Rarotonga with that sort of family. And then all her boyfriend. She must have half the town.' Porora laughed reminiscently, her good humour restored. 'She dirty like a mynah, she caw caw when she open her mouth.'

Grace marched without speaking into the wash-house and swept fiercely at all the corners until the dust hung in the air. She could never find words to express that sort of rage.

'You angry with me?' Porora's bulk darkened the doorway as she peered in penitently. 'Oh Gracie. And then you was such a little girl to come into my shop and buy your mother's cigarettes. Only up to here, that little head,' and she showed Grace on the wall. 'You think I don't love you enough? All I say is what everyone on this whole damn island say. Better you know than all those damn smiles of people lying to your face.'

'Excuse me, Porora,' Grace said, her head down, 'I'm trying to sweep around Joe's mattress.'

Sometimes she hated the bulk of her, the smell of coconut oil in her pores, her sleepy malicious face, but only because she also loved her like a mother, helplessly, with no reserves. She swept on and said nothing. It was nearly time to go home.

When she finally came up the track of her house she was panting from the exertion and the heat. She saw people sitting out on the verandah, her mother and two men. She bowed her head wondering if she had time to dash for it to her bedroom, or failing that, take off for the water gardens before they saw her. Her mother was too quick, she caught sight of her and called out across the garden. She was full on, husky with malice.

'Gracie! Your beau's here!'

He was sitting there beside Raoul and Mara, they were like judges on a panel with the blur of their white faces turned towards her. Jack was leaning back on the rotten canvas chair with a drink in his hand. He looked slightly bemused as if he had been hearing extraordinary things.

'Hello,' he said and his voice made her happy again. 'I've just come.'

'You didn't tell me,' Mara said to Grace ambiguously. 'From Auckland too, and over here for a few weeks.'

Raoul stayed uneasily silent, both he and Grace knew her tone of voice.

'Business or pleasure, Jack?' Mara asked, turning to him.

'Both, probably,' he said, his eyes on Grace as she climbed up the steps towards him. He gave her his private smile.

'Now what can that mean? Raoul, have you any idea?'

'No madam,' said Raoul warningly. 'You are Nouvelle-Zelandais?' he asked. 'You have business in this bloody island?'

'Yes, I'm doing research.'

'Research. How interesting, Jack. Researching the locals, are you?'

He smiled at her appreciatively. 'No. I'm doing a survey of agricultural sprays, pesticides in the Pacific, the effects of overdosing on the soil, whether there's dangerous handling.'

'Oh really,' said Mara. 'A bleeding heart sort of job.' She took a sip of sherry. 'I was hoping you'd be some sort of executive, a professional.'

'A savage image,' Jack said placidly. 'Bleeding heart.'

Even Mara had to smile, faintly, at such calmness.

'How sad,' she said. 'A nice young man like you thinking he can save the world. Opening the frig to take out a fresh lettuce and still mourning the passing of the spirit.'

Grace said, 'Let's go, Jack.' For want of something else to do she began to hum.

'Pardon, Grace? Did you say something?' Mara was

pretending to be half asleep with the heat. She lay supine on the sofa swathed in the folds of her rusty black housecoat like a faded movie star.

'I'm humming. The Dead March,' she said, not looking at her mother.

'I can feel it right through your back,' Jack said. He had his cool hand on her. 'It's like telephone wires setting up a hum with the wind.'

'I say,' Mara said. 'This is most distressingly intimate, isn't it? And somehow asexual. Telephone wires? God, Gracie, you're going to find him heavy weather.'

There was a short silence.

'You're not someone I would get especially close to, Mara,' he said. 'But there's no reason why we can't be friends.'

'I have no friends here,' she said, 'and my name is Mrs Starr. With two r's. Now excuse me. I have a huge bubble in my chest. I must go and bring it all up as I know to my cost.'

Raoul gave a small elegant shrug to them both as if to draw their attention to the uniqueness of this woman in spite of her peculiar ways, and helped her tenderly out of the chair. They went inside, leaving behind her special scent, cigarette smoke and sherry mixed with roses. Ever since Grace could remember, her mother had had that sweetish smell clinging to her; as a small girl she would sniff it, greedy for her, lost in admiration.

'That's what you're like,' he said, his hand still on her back. 'I've been trying to think. Water. You're so fresh and clear and quiet. I was wondering what it was.'

She smiled at him.

'I tracked you down,' he said. 'I have to admit it. I found out who you were by asking people. You are Grace the Silent, the most beautiful, creamy, dreamy white girl on the island. I saw you walking along the road one morning, and lying under the tree, and in your paradisical bar. And each time I saw you it was like a rush to the head.'

'I noticed you as well. Of course. You were on the high road, ready to knock me over.' She moved her bare leg against his. They sat silent for a while, not moving again, gazing out into the trees, their bodies close. The heat engulfed them. Only butterflies were moving, floating and tilting in the heavy currents. It was like going up a warm brown tropical river, the trees pulsing and glittering on its banks, travelling slowly together through the afternoon.

'So what are we going to do now?' he asked, touching her face. 'Our boldness is astounding. We hardly know each other. Can you remember us last night?'

'I like hearing you talk,' she said. His hands were like flames on her skin.

'I'm Irish. That's why I talk so nice.' When he smiled he showed white male teeth with a gap on either side. It was a smile full of desire and knowingness, his lips and teeth shone with delicate spittle.

'Would you like to go up to your bedroom? It would be cooler inside and there's probably a soft bed in it and windows into the garden. And everything.'

'I could listen to you forever,' she said.

SIX

'I've never talked to a man who didn't have a hidden agenda about me,' she explained to him much later as they lay in the dark talking like old friends. 'That's why it's unusual. You're so unusual.'

'But I have an agenda.'

'Yes, I know. But I know about it. It's my agenda too.'

'What's your agenda?'

'A passionate love affair with a man as beautiful as a dream.'

'God, what a thing to say. Sometimes it's hard to believe you're only seventeen.'

'It's my life. I grew up like a weed. There were never any limits put on my imagination.'

'I realise,' he said. 'But what did you mean about the agenda?'

'Even kind people. Teachers who wanted to rescue me from my life. They always had a considering look in their eyes. Deep down they were itching to know if I was like my mother. There was always a little tremor to their helping hands. Ah Grace, they said, you're wasted here. A bloody rose among thorns.'

'You can see their point, all the same. I admit it, I'm not deep down sure what you're doing here either. Where your sources are, for instance.'

'Oh no. It's nothing to do with that sort of curiosity about a *person*. It's to do with my mother, and sex, the way we live. They knew I had no protection and it brought out their hunting instincts in spite of their best intentions.'

'Old grey men in shorts, long white sox. Blank-faced murderous schoolboys. Fat tourists looking for fun.'

'How did you guess all that?' she asked, pleased.

'Imagination,' he said. 'Imagination and love.'

'The worst ones are the tourists with shorts and flannel hats and big hairy stomachs. I used to have fantasies about being somehow corrupted by them in spite of myself.'

'I can imagine that for some reason. The angel in the corner of the dive, serving beers, with her beautiful ripe body and those grave bedroom eyes. The gross paedophile from Sydney predatory towards this innocent child of the tropics. Little does he know that she is brilliant as well as beautiful, with a mind like a kaleidoscope and unspeakable fantasies of her own.'

'We're already saying terrible things to each other,' she said absently.

'I'm usually such a shy thing with women too.'

'Really?' said Grace politely, looking away from him at the dark tree outside her bedroom window. 'That's a bit hard to believe.'

He said after a while, 'I keep thinking I've known you all my life. It's embarrassing to me that I take liberties with you like this. You say things that I've had reverberating inside my head for years and have never formulated. It's like listening to your most secret thoughts through a megaphone.'

'You have strange points of reference. Telephone wires, megaphones, pesticides. Are you a scientist?'

'Yes and no. I'm the presenter on a little science show for kids. We talk about the planet and pollution and how frogs mate. We give them lots of interesting facts and a laugh or two. I tell the kids to plant trees and recycle paper. But all the time I'm bursting with my secret aim.'

'Which is?'

'I hope to show them, subliminally of course, that we will all die unless they stop watching TV and place their bodies between a living thing and death-bringer.'

'How are you teaching that?'

'By my shining words. I want them to fight the people who are going to destroy the world. I'm too late, and too polite to do anything.'

'I haven't noticed. Any politeness I mean.'

'The trouble is I don't really have the language. As soon as you use certain words like planet or pollution, it debases the actual meaning, they become slogans. The kids turn to "Miami Vice" because they've been taught to despise complications, long processes. And a lot of them are contemptuous of vulnerability or passion because it's too weak for them. They want power.'

'Some of them,' said Grace. 'Here a lot of kids wouldn't know what you were talking about. It's more the way New Zealanders and Australians think. And Americans.'

'You think so? But it'll change. Someone told me that the kids here stay up all night watching video nasties.'

'Yes, yes, I know,' she said impatiently. 'But the *papa'a* won't find it as easy as they think to change things here.'

'You're one of them,' he said. 'Why don't you admit it?'

'I was born here.'

He smiled at her suddenly. 'I still can't believe it. A week ago, Auckland and urban angst, and now this.'

'And so,' Grace said, knowing it had to be said soon before their future nights of love had buried her courage. 'When are you going back to Auckland?'

'Soon. There's Kate, who you saw at the water gardens. I don't usually betray the people in my life.' He was silent for a while. 'I know it doesn't look it.'

'Ah,' she said much more calmly than she felt. 'Married.'

'Not quite but years of love between us,' he said in a sad voice. 'It would be her worst fear. That I would fall wildly in love with a woman like you while she's not with me.'

She said, 'You haven't known me long enough to be able to say things like that.'

'Yes, I have. You have the softest, most clever expression I have ever seen on anyone. All I want to do is be with you and make love to you all the time, and hear you talking in that Rarotongan lilt of yours.'

'This is going to be too complicated.'

'Now and then I stop and realise I've only known you for a few hours and it isn't too late to cut it. But I still don't want to leave you. If you know what I mean.'

'Strangers in lurve,' she said.

'Are you in love too?' he asked. 'Are you?'

Grace got off the mattress and went silently down into the kitchen to get a bottle of sherry. The floorboards groaned, a moving mat of cockroaches whisked clean from the benchtop the minute she switched on the light. When she came back he was leaning out the window, his naked body white in the shadows.

'The Princess in the Tower,' he said, turning, 'and all around the Dark Forest.'

He took the bottle gently from her and drank, his head thrown back.

'Jesus, that tasted like meths!'

'Mara's been drinking that for years. She says it's full of protein.'

'And you?' he asked casually, settling back onto the mattress, his arms behind his head. 'Do you have a boyfriend?'

'No.'

'Ever? What about lovers?'

'A few.'

'A few?'

'Three or four.'

'Did you love them?'

'What is this?'

'I'm jealous. I hate the thought of that soft-mouthed dreamy look being for someone else. Someone touching your skin.'

She laughed in surprise. 'I may have been mistaken about you all along. You could easily be a psychopath.'

'I'm sorry. I've never felt like that before. With Kate. I'm really sorry, Grace.'

'I hope so.'

'Are you still angry?'

'No. Everything is forgiven, or nearly everything.'

'Which parts?' he asked her, urgent, leaning forward to kiss her feet. 'Aren't?'

'I'll tell you later,' she said, her voice already drowsy with the love to come. 'When I know.'

SEVEN

From then on she had a recurring image of herself as a lone swimmer drifting in a bottomless sea, spiralling through acres of green dreaming water, voluptuously suspended. She knew all along that the water around her could crush her heart at any time if she made a false move, that inevitably the pressure of it would gather momentum, send her like a rocket to the surface and burst her through into the light — whether dead or alive didn't trouble her, she floated between possibilities in easy unconcern.

'You've got absolutely no ambition, that's your trouble,' Mara complained. 'At your age I was travelling, studying, setting up to marry the most eligible boy at university.'

'I know. You've told me this before, Mara.'

It was an overcast humid day and mosquitoes whined tinnily in her room, a dreary sign of more rain to come. Mara smelt badly of sherry, her housecoat looked rusty from years of damp. Grace was trying to get dressed and ready for work but she couldn't wake up properly, she stumbled around, too heavy and foggy to set herself clearly in motion.

'Jack's all very well, Grace, but he's a fanatic. He has a very big curriculum in Auckland which doesn't include you. He's a seething old cauldron, that one. And what's happened to his girlfriend? That glowing prophet of love of yours?'

'You should ask him. You've never had any inhibitions about asking him anything before, have you?'

'Sent her home probably. He's a manipulator of hearts. He wants her, but he wants his delectable little schoolgirl for a couple of weeks too. You do know what I mean, or don't you?'

'What's all this about schoolgirl? I left school years ago,' Grace said absently, struggling into her skirt. 'What have you got against him?'

'His girlfriend,' Mara insisted. 'That's only one point.'

'He's a loving man. His life overflows with it, that's all.'

'This is disappointing. It reminds me of those photos of young smiling Mormon wives clustering around their husband. You know. He's standing there with a gun and a cowboy hat and there's a glorious feeling of power and perversity, submission in the air.'

'Mara,' Grace said from her fog of sleepiness. 'You're talking too much.'

'You know what I mean though. We forgive him everything, they say. Our souls are his because he is a god among men. We are the happiest of women.'

'I've got nothing to forgive him for.'

'Ah, but you will,' Mara said darkly. She got off the chair. 'I'm only trying to warn you for your own good. You forget. I've had decades of experience. Of all the nuances, mind you.'

'Never,' Grace said, picking up her straw hat. 'I never forget your decades because they're mine, all mine.'

'I seem to have very little influence over you any more,' Mara said, walking to the door. 'It's not a good thing.'

At the Paradise, Grace did nothing, she sat at the bar with her head on her arms, a faraway smile on her face. Since she'd met Jack, her skin was always tender and tingling, as if she had just stepped out of a bath. Every night, hours before closing time she would start the waiting for him, so intensely, that his final arrival almost became an anti-climax. She pretended to herself that he was only a man like the others, that his presence did not disturb her, but all the time she was waiting smilingly for the moment of contact. It only took a certain soft appraising look from him, a movement of the hands, a smile for her to know him again.

It was a ritual. She watched him from the kitchen and thought to herself, that beautiful stranger over there was the man who shared her bed every night, it was that face which turned so stern and absorbed above her in the dark, those hands which had such startling gifts. That quiet man over there desired her completely, had seemingly endless wanton need of her, she would think to herself, smiling, possessing him heartlessly once again without his knowledge. All the time Jack sat there unconscious of the liberties she was taking, slightly bored, thinking his own thoughts as he waited for her.

'Your boyfriend here,' Porora whispered, her mouth so close Grace felt the warm spittle pricking at her, her rich breath. 'That Jack of yours.'

When Porora was not there Grace made the last drinkers go right on time. Half grumbling, half indulgent they slid off their stools with the startled disgruntled dignity of hens pushed off a perch. She had never enforced closing time before, just leaned against the bar along with them until they stopped drinking and stumbled out into the night.

The season of tropical downpours had started, the sky always looked bruised with the weight of the thunder. It was like the skin of a rotten fruit ready to burst. The rain when it came, didn't cool the air, only charged it with more moisture. Walking home was like swimming together in an invisible clammy sea. They arrived at the house, sweaty, silent from tiredness and sat out on the verandah in the shadows, drinking and listening to the owls calling in the ghostly trees. The ease between them made her feel extra-ordinarily light, as if the burden of her strangeness had been lifted, she was freed from the judgements of other people and herself for the first time, by his glowing approval. Her distance from people, the Princess Anne syndrome, was burnt away by the fire between them.

Up in her bedroom, musty-smelling from nights of sex, there was no need for her to guard against possible hurt. The two of them had staked out a private domain of darkness and release, where anything was permissible and each night was like a journey further into a cave. Grace started to believe seriously that no one else had ever explored such extremes of pleasure before. Sometimes when they were making love, she secretly watched his face, deathly pale, eyes closed, mouth twisted in a rictus of pain and ecstasy, and she felt guilty at intruding on such suffering intensity, and exultant about her power over him. Remote and silent he moved beneath her like a willing victim, the curls around his head lying on the pillow like a crown. Afterwards as they lay drenched, drowned, all boundaries between them vanished away in the torrent, his expression was as clear and serene as a child's. Sometimes he was too urgent to speak, opening her legs with brusque hands, settling himself astride her and inside her, making himself and her ready for another long blind ride in the dark. She would think smilingly, not again, but then those few seconds of superiority passed and she was gone, lost again, crooning and groaning out her pleasure, her open mouth on his skin, face against his thumping heart. She was amazed at the sounds which came from her involuntarily while they were making love, she heard herself screaming, weeping, moaning and wailing like a fishwife, urgent, primitive noises like pleas for help, laments, cries of pain and love.

'I'm my mother's daughter,' she said once apologetically. 'I've never been so caught up in it before.'

'But I love it,' Jack said, stroking her white haunch as she lay on her side facing him. 'It feels as if you're singing in my ear all the time. It makes me feel all-powerful. I touch you, you sing.'

She laughed and took his hand lovingly. 'You're not scared of anything, are you?'

'She walks in beauty like the night,' he said. 'I can't stop looking at your face. It's a terrible curiosity.'

'You look at the rest of me with a more terrible curiosity than that.'

'I try not to, Grace. You may be your mother's daughter but I am the Pope's son. I have a healthy respect for sin and guilt.'

'Ah Jack,' she said. 'Jack the priest taking the sacrament with his lovely carnal hands.'

'It's much better with guilt,' he said, stroking her. 'Guilt's given me a real shivery edge, reservoirs of energy built up after years of boyhood terror. I'd never have been able to fully express my lust for you if it hadn't been for the nuns. Bless them. Flicking at my person.'

'Did they really? Flick at you?'

'No,' he said, 'but they looked at me in disgust and I knew they could see right into my wicked heart. It was too much for a sensitive boy who only wanted to dream of sex day and night.'

They hardly slept because of the heat and their preoccupation with each other, they lay night after night light-headed with exhaustion, listening to the rain clattering on the roof. When it wasn't raining and the weather was not too sticky they walked, to the Takuvaine water gardens, up the vanilla-smelling path to Te Rua Manga, along the dreamtime beaches where a tricky little breeze rattled the palm trees, and waves of white-legged tourists picked their way over the sand looking intently for shells and hoping for a miracle.

They went up to the Ara Metua, the ancient road surrounded by land that had been cultivated for a thousand years. It was fresh and moist up there, sheltered by carefully planted trees. There were fragrant patches of pawpaw, mangoes, tomatoes, dry taro laid out by the roadside, squares of earth surrounded by banks of green. It always seemed deserted and whenever she went up there Grace imagined that the people who had just been working in a field the minute before she came had silently disappeared into the trees at the sound of her footsteps. Once she caught a glimpse of a group of people sitting close together under a tamanu tree and the murmur of their voices floated across to her like music. There were a few small houses tucked away behind the banana palms, scrawny chooks scratching the earth, the sound of streams hidden in the trees, a feeling of secret abundant life.

The fragrance of smoke hung in the air and in the dusk the hibiscus glowed like the bonfires of leaves farmers had set on the hillside. The ancient road was soft as sand underfoot. Jack was preoccupied that night and hardly noticed where she led him.

'I'm like another white official,' he kept saying sombrely. 'That's all. They're polite, they smile but their eyes are disbelieving. I saw a group of people really hoeing into a clump of weeds with the spray, right beside a patch of taro. They'll start to get sick and no one will know why. The companies have already made their money, they've sold the sprays and people see that they work. Bang. Another weed dead.'

His white shirt glimmered in the half-light as he walked beside her. It reminded her of their first walk together, the same long silences, the electric anticipation between them.

'You look like a ghost. A walking incandescence.'

'Are you interested in this?' he asked tenderly. 'The survey? The poisons of the Western world?'

'Yes. But I've got a different approach. I haven't got your charisma. I couldn't lead people over the fiery plains like you.'

'Fiery plains?' he smiled down at her in surprise. 'I never thought of myself like that.'

'Something to do with the light anyway. What does Mara call you? The glowing prophet of love.'

'Sarcastically of course.'

'Of course. But she knows it's true.'

She kissed his hand without looking at him and they were both suddenly embarrassed.

'Your mother talks like an Old Testament prophet. She's so full of dire warnings and admonitions. No wonder you can talk about fiery plains so easily. No wonder it falls off your tongue.'

'Porora's even worse,' she said, smilingly at the thought. 'Actually she might be able to help you with the sprays.'

'What?' he asked, still thinking his own thoughts.

'Porora. She could arrange a meeting of people just like that.' As soon as she said it, she half-regretted the impulse. A vision of Porora, monstrous, insolent, her hands grasping the pineapple machete, rose before her like a terrible warning. 'She'll like you. She likes pretty men.'

'She sounds as if she eats people. And what's this "pretty"?'

'You're a sex object, aren't you? To me you are.'

'So you've been using me all this time,' he said turning to look at her.

'I've been using you all this time. The man I adore is going out with a whore.' There was a silence. 'That's Kate's song,' she added and then was ashamed.

'Don't say it,' Jack said. 'Please. If you don't want to go on with it, I promise I'll stay away. I'm not a shit.'

'I know that,' she said, 'it's useless to talk about it.'

They turned down a side road leading back to the sea, where a grove of coconut palms grew in stately lines down the hill and a few goats tethered to the skinny trunks turned to gaze after them.

'We could live in one of those,' Grace said, making it worse for herself. 'If things were different.'

She pointed to the houses they were passing, all of them empty, rotting among the trees, the owners long gone to New Zealand, Australia, America. Some of them were half-collapsed, overgrown with vines; mynahs gathered to feed on the pulpy fruit left to liquify in the front gardens, thin green lizards dozed on their sagging walls.

It began to rain, an unexpected shower in the warm twilight and with one accord they both began to run fast, as if they were escaping from the approaching deluge.

EIGHT

Porora was sitting at home in her lounge fanning herself and watching a video when they arrived. It was a bare elegant Rarotongan room with photographs on the walls covered with plastic *eis*, shell ornaments, the floors covered with springy grass-smelling mats, the scent of flowers through the open windows. There was no trace of Joe's presence there except for one faded photograph of their wedding, his white starveling face looking incongruous among the broad brown ones of her own family.

She stood up, smiling graciously. She was wearing a velvety hibiscus in her ear as if she was expecting them.

'Grace, you didn't warn me we have company. I don't know what food I have in my kitchen.'

'Never mind,' said Grace.

'Ah never mind she say, Jack. Never mind. A tall man like you needs something, eh?' They stood awkwardly in the room while she moved off to the kitchen, stately in her displeasure. The video was some horror film, people with blank zombie faces were staring directly into the camera.

'Shit,' whispered Jack. 'This is *The Terminator.*' They sat down on the sofa side by side and watched silently. After a few minutes Grace went into the kitchen.

'Can I help?' she asked. 'What are you doing in here?'

There were plates of cold chicken, jellies, a cake, some taro, bottles of cordial, mango and pawpaw all over the bench, flies buzzing above them. Porora was in an apron chopping up a pineapple.

'You going to marry him?' she whispered fiercely indicating him with her head.

'He has a girlfriend,' she said sombrely, 'back home in New Zealand. He's going back.'

'That's nothing,' Porora said, chopping again. 'You never like your bloody boyfriends before, not like this one. He suit you. Now carry this in. You never get a man like that, always standing around dreaming, your face so silly, and dark under your eyes like that.'

Grace took the dishes in her hands meekly and half smiling went out into the sitting room.

'Here, here,' hissed Porora, bringing out a card-table and spreading a white starched cloth on it.

'What's this!' said Jack, standing up eagerly. 'Food!'

Porora laughed with pleasure, wiping her hands on her apron and turning the plates this way and that, putting her big hands on the food to rearrange it.

'He's a hungry man,' she said. 'Wearing yourself out with sexing.'

'That's true,' Jack said calmly, loading up his plate. 'This is delicious. Delicious. You having some Grace? Home-cooked food.' He had the absorbed expression of a greedy boy.

They sat eating, their eyes straying to the TV every now and then.

'That's a pretty rabid film that,' he remarked, his mouth full.

Porora laughed, not really listening to him, she was watching him eat. She didn't touch anything herself, she hovered, offering more food, nudging Grace.

'Why don't you have something to eat too?' asked Grace irritated. She had never seen Porora so effusive.

'So, you want to marry Grace?'

'I'd like to.'

'Why don't you stay here? Your girlfriend stop you?'

'Yes,' he said calmly.

'You're lucky she even look at you,' Porora said, ignoring Grace's frown. 'She don't like men. All the time I tell her to go out with this one and that. Rich boys, boys from New Zealand, Australia. I tell her she get old and no one want her and then she have no money.'

He looked over at Grace, smiling so tenderly that she wanted to go and lie against him, her head on his warm stomach.

'Her mother she have many many men. I pray to God sometimes for her. My daughter all married, good husbands, children for me. But Grace? Nothing. Working in my bad place. Sleeping, reading. This is a good girl.'

'Yes,' said Jack. 'She's the most beautiful woman I've ever seen.'

Porora smiled secretively.

'Jack is doing research here,' Grace said, glaring at her. 'On the sprays they use to kill weeds and insects. He says they're poisonous, they poison the earth and the food.'

'Oh?' said Porora. 'You a Health Inspector?'

'No,' said Jack. 'It's nothing official.'

'Why do you do this then? Those sprays work and quicker than the bloody hoes. How can the government sell those poisons here, if that's so?' She was very interested.

'Well, the problem is that even they have only just found out how poisonous they are. They didn't know before.'

'OK. Give me some of your papers about it. Now, you're not eating this chicken, Jack. Have some chicken for your skinny little stomach. You need some building up for the next few days.'

'Porora's a local healer. And my second mother as well,' Grace explained as they walked home afterwards, bloated and queasy from all the food. 'I've never seen her so nice to anyone before. I told you.'

'She didn't seem that interested in the survey.'

'You've just got to take time over things like that. You can't draw attention to yourself here. That's why she's so noncommittal. They know she's not in the comfortable eccentric category. You can't just laugh at her and leave her alone.'

'What do you mean?'

'See that half-built motel over there? All along the coastal strip there are ancient burial grounds. That's why the road's called Ara Tapu. In the old days, she told me that people lived around the Ara Metua away from the wind and they buried their people down by the sea. Now the companies are just building over the bones. I saw them myself. They don't even bother to move them. Porora's the only person who's said anything.'

'Well I suppose that's fair enough. Old human bones are excellent for strengthening foundations. Give them sustenance, form, especially for such a spiritual project as a motel.'

'She won't go past there any more. She thinks she's let them down. She has terrible dreams.'

'But can't anyone stop them?'

'The locals are not happy, but the building company said it was the European way.'

'You know, it's strange,' he said. 'There's a polite and total conspiracy of silence here. I don't know whether it's indifference or whether people have learnt through bitter experience never to be open to whites. I suppose they've had centuries of loony missionaries. And now it's the dollar and corruption to take over where they left off.'

'Porora told me about the missionaries. They used to beat teenage girls because they laughed on Sundays. Her own mother. They tied them to trees.'

'Well, you can't blame them. It must have been horrible to hear that godless laughter when they were trying to bury that sort of paganism forever. They probably thought they'd succeeded.'

'Maybe. It's most probable that the *papa'a* are too involved in other things to see what's going on underneath.'

'What about you? You're a *papa'a*.'

'Maybe.'

'Don't you get angry about what happens here?'

'Sometimes. But that's only because I can see the other side of it. Me being angry has no weight anyway because most white people just think we're beneath notice. I used to get into fights at school because of Mara. The kids hated her because she was so strange. The adults because she's betrayed her class. And she was never apologetic.'

'I know what you mean.'

'But I have a few friends,' Grace said. 'Porora. Raoul.'

'It's strange,' Jack said. 'You're so white-skinned and yet you talk like a Rarotongan sometimes. And think like one.' He sniffed her. 'And you have the same smell.'

'It's not strange. I've lived here all my life. What smell?'

'Scenty things. Coconut oil, sand, frangipani. It's incredibly beautiful. How could anyone find you beneath notice?'

'Only some of them. The ones Mara offended.'

That night Grace dreamt that she was airborne, drifting around above the ground with the butterflies, her hair blowing in the wind. Then the dream changed gear, shifted, she was back on earth and a man had come up behind her to stroke her bare back. She could not see his face, but she could feel the loving strength in his hands. She opened up to the flooding sweetness of it, his breath in her hair, the pressure of his hands. It was like a ritual, in the dream she stayed absolutely still, even when his hand slowed and came to rest with calm authority between her legs. She woke herself with an orgasm, she was on fire, disoriented by her dream and her powerful reaction to it.

In the bare bedroom, bone-white with the light of the moon, his sheets flung off, he was still there beside her, his stern sleeping face, the curves of his body as perfect as marble. She gazed down at him marvelling at his trust as he slept like a carnal little boy in her bed, his cock hanging softly between his thighs. She lay back on the mattress, unable to sleep for love, listening to his breathing, night birds calling outside like ghosts, the faint, wild cracking of the palms. She had never felt so comforted by one single thing before, his presence there, his quiet breathing in the room.

NINE

'So why do you keep coming?' Mara asked him impatiently some time after they met. 'Surely you can see you're not wanted?'

They had all been sitting out on the verandah drinking for hours, watching the heavy curtains of rain pouring from the gutters above them on the roof.

'Not by you maybe. Although deep down of course I think there's a different story going on.'

'It's your idealism I find so grating.' She lay back on the damp old sofa and lit a cigarette. 'God knows how Grace puts up with it.'

'But why does it grate? You should be proud to have such a stubbornly optimistic person around here.'

'People like you should be made to see how the world really works. It's nothing to do with ideals. A handshake here, money passing hands there. That's all. Survival, then death.'

'Anything can *survive*. That's nothing. Even the rats on Enewetak Atoll. The place is so crawling with radiation it'll take twenty-five thousand years to decontaminate, and there they are running around, happy as sandboys, their sleek little hides bursting with goodness.'

'I can't bear the way you nuclear people have all these bogus figures. Twenty-five thousand years. What does that mean?'

'I read it,' Jack said pensively, gazing out into the garden in drunken melancholy, 'in the *Cook Islands News*.'

'The trouble is people like you deep down want an apocalypse now so that in the last righteous minute you can say I told you so. But none of us are going to die tragic deaths. We'll just get older and more boring and die of something festering and God will punish us like that.'

'Well that's disappointing to me, Mara. You're just one of the millions who've let the iron wheels of the '80s crush their heart. I'm disappointed. I thought for sure you'd have brilliantly original reasons for being a cynic. Especially in a place like this.' He looked around at the house and the dripping jungle for a moment. 'But there you are, you're just like any other self-serving businessman who opens his paper every morning and curses the world. Wake up to it, boy! The world will eat you alive if you don't get in there first! That's my father talking, by the way.'

'A nasty drunk,' said Mara, impressed in spite of herself. 'And deeply confused. I've always been suspicious of such glowing unremitting niceness. There's usually a septic sore somewhere.'

'But Mara, listen. Forget all this hostility,' he pleaded, his eyes moist with drunken dishonesty. 'We could be friends. We could sit here in the forest telling stories, swapping homespun philosophies. Laughing together over the state of the world.'

'He's become too familiar with me,' she said to Grace. 'I should never have allowed it to go so far.'

'But I want to explain my case to you. I know you're knowledgeable about certain things, but you won't let on.'

'I'm not knowledgeable. All I know is I've no desire to hear about your sloppy wellsprings. Your rats.'

'I honestly don't believe you mean that. Look at you, sitting here on this rotten verandah, your aristocratic blood rotting in your wicked old veins. What have you ever done to justify your life? Except produce Grace? You know we all have to do something authentic at least once in our life. You of all women. It's a simple requirement of existence. Look at my people. They produce authentic images from acts of love which will sear your eyeballs and burn out your brain.'

'What is he talking about?' Mara asked Grace.

'Greenpeace. That's what we do. Traffic in images. It's all we have, the simplicity itself is powerful enough. People in toy boats, washing against the bows of monolithic ships to stop the sailors throwing nuclear waste into the sea, shielding the bloodstained bodies of baby seals from the hunters, sailing yachts under the shadow of a nuclear ship. They are images of the last real heroes of a dying planet. There is no defence against them. The act and the image. Perfect fucking fusion.'

'Language,' murmured Mara, closing her eyes.

'People recognise the real thing — it hits them like a blow to the heart. When I first saw them on TV I knew they were the rainbow warriors. They were giving their lives in front of our eyes to save the planet. Out of love. Nothing more.'

'A spiritual revelation from the flickering screen. Almost total egotism,' she said with her eyes closed. 'I like it.'

'An act of love,' insisted Jack drunkenly. 'An authentic act of love.'

'I honestly believe,' Mara said, still talking to Grace, 'that he's going to quote Che Guevara. You know — every great revolutionary is motivated by love. It's a dreadful thing to say, but I see no alternative.'

'Oh Mara,' groaned Jack, holding his chest. 'You would disembowel for the sake of a *bon mot.*'

'He was going to,' she said. 'There's no doubt in my mind. Oh love sweet love,' she sang tremulously as if it was a hymn.

'I wasn't, Mara,' Jack said. 'But it's never far from my mind.'

'In one way it's sad. Your one-man fight against pesticides in a godforsaken little island. Your megalomania. Sad in one way.'

He laughed suddenly, straightening up as if he were shaking her off.

'Preventing the poisoning of the Pacific may not seem important to you Mara, with your eyes on the real world. Even setting aside the question of social importance, I have to ask you, where has it led me?'

'Where has what led you?'

'To Grace. It has led me to Grace. It's made me worthy of her. I've received the ultimate sacrament from your daughter's hand. I am a man drowning in bliss. I'm lost in the great white whale of the Pacific, the most perfect whale in the universe.' He stretched out in front of Grace as she sat silently listening, his face muffled in her lap, his arms around her waist like a drowning man. 'But I'm lying, Grace, and for this I deserve terrible punishment. There is no actual whale. Idealism, fighting poisons, has led me to a woman of incomparable beauty of soul with hair like gold and the stillness of a mountain pool. A pool reflecting my wicked face.'

Grace stroked him lovingly, lurching a little as she leaned over him.

'He's very well-spoken, isn't he?' Mara said. 'For bog-Irish working class. Just be more careful with our verandah, though, Jack. You've knocked a little hole there with your boot.'

'It's not even yours. It belongs to someone else. You're like a tropical Miss Havisham rotting to death in the jungle with rotgut sherry and your bridal finery in rags and your cold judgements. You've deluded yourself into thinking this house is yours.'

'That's not totally true,' Grace said, finally moved to speech. 'Mara might seem grotesque, but she's not stupid or ugly. Miss Havisham was terribly stupid. Like a stubborn old peasant. Stupidly resentful.'

Jack stared at her, momentarily thrown. 'I'm still not used to the way your mind works sometimes,' he pleaded at last.

'It's strange,' Mara said. 'People never know how to take it. Literate poor, well-read scum, whatever you want to call us. It offends people's sense of the world. They see it as a terrible affront. Especially idealists.'

'My mother was a scholar and a gentlewoman in her youth,' Grace said, articulating the words carefully, formally. 'She went to university and studied things. We are no fools us. We have a life of our own.'

'I know,' he said. 'I know. I'm sorry. It's just that I've never met anyone like you two before. I need all my energy and imagination just to keep up. It's worth it, but it sometimes becomes — hallucinatory.'

'Give the man a little drink,' Mara said, softening towards him for the first time. 'He does try very hard. I'll give him that.'

'Not *very* hard,' said Jack quickly.

'And so earnest about saving the unsavable. Why should you want to save the world? That's what I can never understand.'

'Because of Grace, for one thing. Who in their right mind wouldn't want to save Grace?'

'That's exactly what I mean about you. That sort of thing is so impressive to a young girl. I don't want you to undermine Grace by that easy impressiveness of yours. That promiscuous energy.'

'There's no pleasing the woman,' he said, giving Grace a smile. 'There's nothing I can do.'

'Grace understands more than you think. She'll live in this place forever, she'll be a stayer and people will come to her for lost information. Contrary to appearances, Jack, I'm not the witch here.'

Her voice trailed off into the breathless heat. Above them, ropes of thick cobwebs hung from the struts and fat black spiders moved silently into their line of vision and settled themselves to wait. It had stopped raining for a while and the wood of the verandah smelt like fishing boats and the sea.

'I've never heard you talk like that about me before,' Grace said, with a little warning edge to her voice.

'And another thing,' Mara said. 'You're the only person she's loved as much as she loves me, so you're extremely privileged.'

'I know. But why does everyone speak for you, Grace? Porora and Mara, the twin priestesses guarding the shrine.'

'The dog-faced goddesses more likely,' said Mara. 'Porora is a wicked old woman wreathed in unspeakable mysteries and I too am almost past my prime, alas. But we both know purity when we see it.'

Grace stood up, suddenly irritated. 'Let's go, Jack. It's not that I don't appreciate you,' she said to Mara. 'But sometimes I could break your alkie bones when you're playing all your little games against Jack.'

'What little games?' Mara asked, aggrieved, lighting a cigarette. 'Where are you going?'

'To work.'

'It's early, isn't it?'

'Yes,' Grace said, 'but I need some air.'

'Is it true?' Jack asked later. He was lying spreadeagled on the grass staring up into the leaves. It had started to rain again, lightly, and drops of water glistened on each heart-shaped leaf of the taro growing below them in the pool. The soft greyish light, the ancient teitei trees shading the shining pools, the falling water, were like a landscape she had glimpsed before in a dream, or in another life. In her pleasant drunken haze, its familiarities and harmonies were infinitely soothing.

They spoke to each other with the exaggerated care of the quietly drunk.

'That you could break her alkie bones?'

'Sometimes it's the only language she understands,' Grace said. 'I have to stop her for her own good.'

'What about your own good?'

'There's that too.'

Jack's hair glistened and curled with the rain, he lay back heavily disregarding the wet grass.

'Such violent talk. Break your alkie bones.'

'She's like a lion, my mother. I have to use extreme measures. Cracking whips, flame-throwers. Or she'll eat me.'

She lay back on his chest. They were enclosed by the wall of water as it fell through the hills and filled up the ancient pools, mingled with the soft sigh of the rain.

'I dream about you. Painful hard-working dreams full of rooms and people breathing behind me.'

'What's happening in them?'

'You're often sitting there and I can't get you to come with me. There was a horrible one last night about passages and trying to pull you through, but you were too heavy.'

'Oh yes?' she said, lying back on the wet grass and smiling sloppily up at the leaves. 'That's not very nice.'

'Well it's true. I prefer you in front of me. When you're not there or I'm just dreaming about you there are always anxieties at the back of my mind. I have to see you quickly to be comforted.'

'My dreams about you are always very immediate. For instance, the other night I dreamt that I followed the line of your spine all the way down with the tip of my tongue, and then I turned you over.'

'What for?' he asked, becoming warmly interested.

'To see if you had an erection as I hoped.'

'I like this place,' Jack said getting up and shaking his hair so that drops flew all over the grass. 'But it's not wet enough.' He looked over at her, smiling. He was suddenly as lithe and warm and quick as a cat. 'Why don't we go into the jungle?'

She thought of the narrow shady paths up there, worn so deep by generations of patient feet that they were half underground. Surrounded by banks of shining green soft enough to lie on.

'I know a place. If you want absolute total wetness. And acts of love.'

'Yes,' he said. 'I do.'

TEN

'I looked at that stuff that boy give me,' Porora said to Grace that night. 'About them sprays. I think I'm going to call a meeting. He's got some warnings, that boy of yours.'

Joe said to her from across the bar where he was sitting reading the newspaper, 'Get off it will you, Porora. You're always sticking your nose into things. I heard about that motel as well.'

'What did you do?' asked Grace. The two of them stood against the bar, smoking lazily, gazing off into space.

'You tell her. Causing trouble, telling boys to stop work just because of old bones. She's always going on about them. Drives me nuts.' He looked sick and uneasy as if even the shadowy light in the bar was too much for his eyes.

'That bloke of yours, Grace. He's just as bad. Coming in here with his pretty face. Stirring up trouble. The farmers are not too happy about it. They reckon he's a Communist.'

'Ah Joe,' Grace said, smiling at him.

'But what's it got to do with him?' Joe asked heatedly. 'You tell me that, eh Gracie girl. What's in it for him? Too baby-faced for his own good, thinks he's god almighty come to teach us yokels.'

He jealous, that old boy,' Porora said with her malicious flicker. 'He mad. He don't like this man sexing with his pet. His Gracie girl.'

'This one don't even go to church,' said Joe, furious, slapping at the newspaper with his trembling old hands. He kept his head down, trying to control his rage. 'You ask the other women. Her mates. She never goes to church. She's a bloody witch doctor.'

Grace went out the back to sweep the yard. She had recently started to feel uneasy about the quarrels between Porora and Joe. When they were together there was an evil feeling in the air as if they would will each other to die if they had the chance, there was a trembling on the brink of all kinds of old married madness between them.

'He's gone!' Porora called. 'Grace! That man! Come in here!'

She went back in, slowly carrying the broom. She was still slightly drunk, her clothes damp from lying in the grass with Jack, the nerves of her skin still sensitive, and she didn't feel like being involved in anything harsh.

'He going mad with the booze,' said Porora, 'and other things.' She wiped the glasses, watched Grace smilingly.

'Do you love him?'

'Him?' she laughed outright with her rich contemptuous laugh and made a chopping gesture with her hand. 'He's a drunk, *kona* all the time, he's got no spirit. One day I like to crack him in half,' she said.

'You didn't tell me about the men at the site,' said Grace hurriedly.

'I know that. You got your own battles to fight.'

'Like what?'

'You got your mama, you got Jack, you got them sprays.'

'That's nothing,' said Grace.

'People come secretly to me at night,' she said. 'They want me to do something. See the *papa'a* think of me like this.' She pointed her thumb down aggressively, pulled the corners of her mouth downwards. 'Me, running this bad place, old New Zealand drunk mens here every day, my husband no good. Fat boys for sons. But my own people know who I am. My *mamaruau*, my *tupuna*.'

She moved gracefully from out behind the bar, she sailed like a ship in the shadows. Grace was entranced by her size, her deadly intelligence, those terrible eyes of hers that dispensed justice and death in one stony glance.

'I've got to go, Gracie. Look after this will you? I've got some other things to do.'

Porora and Joe were increasingly leaving the running of the place to her as they went their separate ways. Grace liked being there on the quiet nights, there was not much to do, and everyone was silent and private as if they were all in a trance. By the end of the night the last customers were sorrowfully drunk, leaning on the bar as if they were praying for deliverance, old men rotted out from the ease and despair of life in the tropics, dreaming of New Zealand with its clean tin roofs and corner dairies, the crisp clear luminescence of its sky. The air was full of their inarticulate longings. On nights like that the Paradise was strange and timeless as a dream, it was like all the tiny bars found in remote corners of the world, a place of comfort and despair for the lonely, the displaced, the powerless drifters who mouldered their lives away there, drinking and dreaming of home.

ELEVEN

The night of the meeting was steaming hot, it was building up to a storm and in the tiny Scout hall with its stained walls and pictures of the Queen the people in the audience fanned themselves and moved restlessly. The sweaty smell was overpowering until Grace stood up and pulled open the double doors at the back, letting in the smell of damp leaves and the sea. Then a battalion of mosquitoes forced her to get up and pull them shut again. About twenty men sat in a circle of wooden chairs, they were all working men, Rarotongan, Porora's circle of middle-aged and elderly family connections. They sat in their work clothes, big hands resting easily between their thighs, faces ahead as if they were in church. The only woman besides Grace was Porora, she sat in the front row beside Jack, a huge white straw hat shadowing her face, wearing a frilly scarlet Mother Hubbard which glowed flamboyantly in the dark little hall. Her face was impassive as she got up to introduce Jack, deepened into contempt as she gazed around at the small audience. Jack stood up to speak next. Freshly shaved, his hair slicked back with water, dressed in white cotton pants with his shirt sleeves rolled loosely on his brown arms, he was a man glowing with love, his aquiline face and tender eyes were sparkling with his message.

The audience stirred and settled, his sincerity was so noticeable that they recognised it immediately. Grace sitting there amongst them felt their smiling appreciation around her. She had a presentiment of loss as she watched him, a fresh realisation of his overflowing heart and her own nature. She knew that his business was out there in the world, and she wasn't even sure what hers was except that it was internal, inarticulate, and seemed to take forever to be showing itself. Different paths, she thought sadly, she could almost see the two tracks stretching out in front of her there in the hall. His figure at the end of the room seemed smaller, bathed in light, he pleaded for grace from the silent listening people, and she watched him intently as if she would never see him like that, so perfect, again.

Porora spoke again after Jack had finished, she stood like a giant, hands at her sides, face emotionless. But her voice was so low and singsong that Grace could only catch the general drift. When she sat down she wiped a tear from her face, roughly, as if she was punishing herself for the weakness of crying.

'What did she say?' whispered Grace to her neighbour.

'She talk about sprays, *ivi o aku tupuna.*' He shushed her importantly with his hands as Jack stood up to ask for questions.

Each of the men stood, one by one and made their own speech in Maori or English, they spoke of things that Grace could tell were not for general knowledge. She realised that Porora and Jack had opened up a Pandora's box of grievances and sorrows about the island in their speeches. It was as if there was a flame leaping in the room. The men spoke about the desecration of the burial grounds, the poisoning of the air and water, the mynahs killing off the old wild birds, the empty houses which stood forsaken everywhere. As they spoke she could see the fear in their faces, that all their shining ancient knowledge would die with them, leaving nothing to counter the fatal flood of seedy delights and poisons engulfing them. An old roadworker who lived in the Takuvaine valley stood up.

'No one has spoken of these things before in public, there are no *papa'a* here who are concerned about these things,' he said. 'But we have met this young man who has travelled from Auckland to tell us this important thing. About the sprays I use every day for the weeds and think it is like water and nearly as harmless to us. We want to thank this man. We appreciate the kindness of his heart!'

He began to sing a hymn and the old men in the hall stood and joined in. Grace felt like a small child again as they sang in their rich grandfatherly voices, their very solidity was a comfort, the song came from certain rituals rooted deep in the past. She was always warmed by the way Rarotongans sang to grace a gathering and give each other comfort, but this time as the sound rose and fell like a wave around her, she felt embarrassed to be listening in, to be witness to such passionate grieving.

Outside the rain had started again, it crashed onto the tin roof like a hail of bullets. Through the windows she could see the rivulets streaming off the heavy fleshy leaves of the umbrella tree as it bowed under the weight of the storm.

TWELVE

'Those bastards,' Porora said fiercely. She was holding a long curved palm leaf over her head for shelter, it trembled and glittered with water as she picked her way delicately along the road. The rain had eased off again, only a thin drizzle fell. Grace's damp dress was clinging to her skin, yet she was sweating as she walked.

'What can they do? Nothing. They all the old ones. Too old for their own good.'

She was going so slowly they had to dawdle to stay with her. She was deep in thought, her shoulders hunched with concentration.

'The meeting went very well,' Grace said to placate.

'Oh them sprays. That's fine about them. That's OK giving them old men the education to pass on. It's my *tupuna* I worry about. That's who I think about all the time.'

Jack said, 'We can do something to help. If you want us to.'

'OK,' Porora said, smiling wolfishly. 'But what happen to them at the present time? Trapped forever under this *papa'a* motel of yours?' She spat on the road. Tears were glistening on her cheeks again.

'Oh Porora,' Grace said helplessly to her.

'Those are my *tupuna*, my loved ones. That's all. I think of their poor bones unloved by us lying in the cold. Them boys pouring the concrete on because they don't know nothing. Only Jesus and money, our kids know about now. I have dreams when they come calling to me, they wake me in the night and I sit up in the dark and cry for them. I can hear their old voices calling to me for help.'

They had reached Porora's house with its fenced concrete tomb in the front garden smothered with bougainvillaea and sprays of artificial flowers. Porora stood there sombrely for a moment, looking down at the ground, her face like stone. Grace felt an ache of love for her as she stood there so unreachable in her grief.

'I'm sorry,' she said. 'You don't deserve this.'

Porora went down the path beside her parents' grave without answering, her massive bulk swallowed up by the shadows of the ironwood tree which grew by her house. The door slammed and the house stayed plunged in darkness. They stood for a while looking after her.

'I hate this place,' said Jack. 'I hate it. It's so lush and innocent but already the corruption is creeping up. It's like a miasma. I can't breathe here. In five years — earlier probably — it'll be like the fifty-second State. Plastic and Reeboks and hidden brutality. You can see the dying of grace already, people like Porora and those old men half-mad with grief. Have you seen Hawaii? Or Fiji since the coup? I couldn't stand it. I'd be deported in six months or become one of those harmless eccentrics you were talking about, one of those guys wearing woollen beanies, with trapped eyes, sounding off in the pub about the CIA. I wouldn't even have Mara's style.'

'It was a good meeting though,' Grace said, frightened. 'It was great.'

'I have to go back to New Zealand,' he said as if he had been practising the words under his breath.

'What?' She had been expecting the blow but still tried to fend it off.

'New Zealand. I was wondering if you would come with me. Come and live with me.'

She had never heard him being so polite. They stood in silence looking at each other.

'Do you have to go now?' she asked. She was astonished at the pain. It was so terrible and grinding she felt as if she had to be alone to attend to it before it became unbearable.

'I want you to come. Please.'

'No, I can't.'

He stood there, watching her, his hair plastered around his skull with the rain so that he looked like a decadent man, impossibly beautiful. Even in the darkness she saw he had gone white. She'd never seen anyone who went so pale. His face completely drained of colour, his eyes went hard and opaque as if all the surfaces had disappeared and no light could glance off his skin.

'That sounds extraordinarily final. Have you been thinking about this?'

'No. For some reason, it's gone right out of my mind. Up until now.'

'Please come with me. I can't live without you.'

She stood listening to him intently.

'What about Kate?' she said finally. It was more a statement than a question. 'The beautiful Kate. With her soft skin. Waiting for you in New Zealand.'

With one accord they started to walk again, heads down. Occasionally a car swished past, the sea below the road boomed wildly in the aftermath of the brief flurry of storm.

'I don't want to walk with you,' she said. 'You go on.'

'What?' He stopped and looked at her in misery. 'Please don't do this, Grace.'

She said stubbornly, 'You go on.'

He lifted up his arms in disbelief. 'It's raining, for God's sake. And late. Let me stay with you.'

'No.'

She heard him give a faint involuntary groan of misery. It was so touching she almost made a movement towards him, but stopped herself in time. He lifted his eyes to her for a minute.

'OK,' he said finally.

She looked after him stunned, as he went slowly up the road. All the defences, little enjoyments, the shining intricate world she had painstakingly built up for herself suddenly seemed almost laughably pathetic beside the shock of his going. She recognised in that instant the terrible authenticity of this real world she had entered, loss and jealously, murderous rage, the sheer voluptuousness of pain. It was a world suddenly dwindled into a streak of sour sky above a long grey plain, a hopeless, heartless existence drained of life. The savageness of it was so unexpected and hateful that she didn't really know what to do except keep moving – she began to walk down the road automatically, drawn in his direction, already rebellious at being held in such bondage. She bent and picked up a stone and held it in her hand, weighing it. Ahead of her was the gloomy shape of the motel against the skyline. It looked like a ruin in its half-finished state, with the beams jutting up crazily into the sky, piles of brick and timber stacked up like fallen stone.

She kept thinking of him in images unbearably sweetened by loss, his warm body weighing on her, the salty smell of his skin, his eyes swollen with love as he lay sprawled beside her, punch-drunk with sex. She thought of the way they used to talk all through the night sometimes, lying in the dark with their eyes ahead like two schoolkids, speaking in soft voices of old painful things, ruminating, trying out their living history on each other in the safe dark.

She walked steadily towards the sea, across the rough ground, tripping on roots and stones, slipping on the muddy grass, and crossed down onto the narrow strip of shadowy beach in front of the motel. It was comforting just to sit on the packed damp sand, hunched over, her legs planted nonchalantly apart like a solitary kid, eyes fixed unseeingly on the water. She threw the stone with a skilful sweep as if she was ten again and practising skipping pebbles.

After a while though the ache became too painful and she had to move again. She started to wander aimlessly up onto the site, kicking at the wood scattered in the grass on the way, finally coming to a stop at the edge of the concrete slab. She stood there looking at it intently as if there was nothing further left to do — she was so disembodied and sluggish with grief.

The slab was grey, smeared and glistening with rain, she bent over and wrote DESECRATORS on it with a muddy stick, then absently smeared it over. As she straightened up ready to move on, a tin of creosote fell from the ledge and a sinister black stain suddenly burst onto the surface of the concrete. She watched it spread slowly and relentlessly, in fascinated horror, half expecting a hand on her shoulder, the growl of a guard dog. But there was only the sound of the wind and rain.

She made the decision then in a muffled remote way, as if she was standing miles away watching herself curiously. Slowly with great care she poured the last few inches of creosote onto the concrete, and then picked up the surveyor's wooden mallet lying by the piles of timber. The thin sheets of cladding were stacked carefully by the builders on bricks set about the wet ground, the factory labels still glued on the surfaces. At that angle it was childishly easy to crack each sheet sharply across the middle.

She worked quietly, the rain lashing her face, stumbling in the mud, scratching her hands in her haste. The sea and the wind in the palms roared at her like friends as she smashed everything delicately and thoroughly with the certainty of a sleepwalker. She felt calm and numb and joyous with the simplicity of her mission.

Taking a thin stick, she wrote carefully on the concrete using the creosote as ink, *Ta te tangata e ruru ra, tana rai ia e kokoti.* What a man sows, he reaps. It was Porora's favourite saying and came to her with all the ease of perfect inspiration. She put the stick down gently when she'd finished and stood up, rubbing her sore back, emptied of emotion. It was only when the headlights of a car swept along the road past the motel that she realised the danger she was in. She looked around at her work, the broken cladding, a heap of glass smashed out from the doors glinting on the creosote-smeared concrete, the innards of an electric saw scattered on the ground. She felt the wicked power of it as she started to walk down the road, the faint flutterings of panic starting up in her stomach at the irrevocability of what she'd done. She looked back again only once, and then began to run effortlessly, as if she was in a dream, half flying along.

When she finally reached the water gardens she was wet through, sweating with exertion, at the limit of her strength. She had never been to Takuvaine at night and the darkness, the velvet sinister grass underfoot, the sobbing of the water were faintly disturbing when she had been expecting only comfort.

As she stood gasping for breath there was a stirring in the shadows and she distinctly saw people moving around casually as if they were old friends too busy to talk. They were working on the channels for the taro, the water flowing under their hands as naturally and peacefully as a waterfall. She stood very still, staring at them — her heart beating loudly, breath stopping in mid-gasp. It was as if in that brief moment, she had been allowed a dazzling glimpse of some mysterious connection she had always half known — between the ancestors Porora grieved over, their work of love at Takuvaine, their bones scattered cruelly on the foreshore.

She closed her eyes, overcome, her breath burning in her chest, and through the darkness of her clenched eyelids she saw them coming, the lost birds, crying and swooping through the trees, their wings flashing in circles of fire.

THIRTEEN

'You was the wrong one,' Porora whispered to her. 'As far as my plans went.' Grace was lying on her mattress with pillows stacked up behind her head. There was a glass jug of lemon drink beside her with ice cubes clinking faintly inside, and a vase with a fragrant bunch of tropical flowers, their sheeny petals already wrinkling and dropping in a velvet pile onto the table.

'That was what I set up for your boyfriend to do. Killing two birds, Grace.'

'What?' she asked uneasily, pretending to be still sleepy.

'It took me a while to make too. It was ready for him to do one fine night. Maybe go to jail, you see? So he stay here for you and make you happy.'

'Porora,' she said sitting up. 'What in God's name are you talking about?'

'It turned out different anyway,' Porora said placidly. 'You done the right thing for yourself and the *tupuna*. You was a real hurricane up there.'

Grace said sharply, 'Don't even talk about it,' but Porora couldn't stop her helpless laughter, the tears started in her eyes with uncontainable mirth.

'That wasn't no peaceful act,' she said, wiping her eyes. 'That wasn't like you with your *papa'a* kindness and all that Greenpeace of your boyfriend's like that.'

'Do you mind?' Grace said, sliding down under the sheets.

She was still floating, in a slightly unreal state, as if she was recovering slowly from a fever.

'You done the right thing, my Gracie. To go straight to the Takuvaine for safety. They were there to look after you. You always did have the right approach I believe. That's why they trusted you.'

'Who trusted me? How did you know I went to Takuvaine?'

'That little Frenchman told me this. He found you on the Ara Tapu wandering like a drunk woman.'

'The Ara Tapu?'

'We don't want to talk no more about that,' Porora said comfortably. 'I just wanted to see if you was OK in here. And you are.' She got up to go. She was dressed in her best outfit, a fitted blue suit which filled the bedroom with musky bulk. The white hat perched on top of her black shining bun made her look terribly tall. For the first time Grace could remember, her expression was soft, she was like a Buddha with that fat serenity, the mirth dancing in her eyes.

'Now you take some days off work if you want, Gracie. You nearly are pale as a *papa'a*.'

She smiled lovingly at her again, her gold tooth flashing.

'Your mama is here,' she added, softly warningly.

'So, Mrs Paulsen. Can you tell me what's wrong with Grace? No one tells me anything.' Mara stood at the doorway. She was dressed but only just. She looked fierce and tousled and hung over.

'She comes home in Raoul's taxi two nights ago, flaked out and hardly breathing, white as a ghost. He doesn't know anything about it either. Is it something to do with that ghastly place of yours?'

'Could be, could be,' Porora answered, dangerously calm, smoothing down one white-gloved hand with the other like a boxer. Mara sat on the sill and lit a cigarette.

'What is it, Grace?' she asked.

'Oh she too tired, Mara. And that Jack going back soon. Back to his girlfriend.'

'Can you tell me yourself? You do look awful enough. Is that what it is?'

'Yes,' said Grace, ignoring Porora's cruel wink.

'Oh God. The forsaken maiden. I warned you, didn't I? I tried to warn you all along. I'm not up to this, Grace, at my time of life.'

'He a fine man,' Porora said. 'He loved the girl better than anyone I know. Except me.' She paused, magnificent in the doorway.

'What would you know?' Mara said, settling luxuriously back against the glass. 'Well, I suppose you do know about love. Of a sorts. After all you do run a brothel. The place was swarming with them last time I went there. What do you people call them? *Taramea*, isn't it? I didn't even like to mention it to Grace.'

'One day,' said Porora, unmoved, 'someone's going to give you a little tap and push you right over. Not me, but someone. You always been a rude woman.'

'Me?' said Mara, genuinely taken aback.

'I have to go now, Grace. Don't you even think of these bad words. They only jealously between us. Nothing more.'

'Jealously?' But Porora was gone before Mara could pounce. Sinister with suppressed malice she moved across to the chair beside the mattress and lit a fresh cigarette with the tip of her last.

'The poor deluded woman. She has ideas above her station, thanks to you. If only I had some money. I'd take you on the plane tomorrow. We could go to Auckland, live in a good suburb. Get away from this decay. All that Graham Greene-type rubbish about the pretty little English rose fading and dying in the tropics, the harsh colonial society crushing women's spirits. It's just masculine mythology about women being weak. All we have to do is go and we've escaped. It's not as if this place is your fate, Grace, your peaks of doom, although you do pride yourself on the drama of all that.'

'Sounds very tempting,' Grace said, looking out the window at Te Rua Manga, purple with a cloud of approaching rain.

'All this intrigue under Pacific skies, mixing with natives. It's gone to your head. You see yourself as a Pollyanna of Rarotonga.'

'You won't know yourself in Auckland either. I can see you at smart coffee parties in your whites, laughing off various insinuations.'

Mara smiled in spite of herself. 'A mean blow from a sick daughter,' she said tenderly for her. 'I know a broken life when I see it, I should hope. I've never been a fool. Do you want something to eat, my child?'

'No.'

Mara's attention suddenly switched, she smiled her special smile of cruelty and exuberance.

'Ah, is that you, Jack?' she called. Grace felt a rush of hope and grief and turned her head to see Raoul coming in the door.

'No, it's only poor Raoul,' Mara said. 'I thought it was Jack delivering the coup de grace. After his dalliance with the nubile schoolgirl, a quick call to the bereaved, and then it's time for the real business of life again. Home and wife and lots of campaigns. But there's always the same old problem. How to explain away the dreamy expression?'

'So how is my little girl?' Raoul asked, bending tenderly over her, his face anxious and cherubic as a schoolboy's. He had brought a spray of scarlet bougainvillaea which he laid on her pillow. 'You were like a white deer in the headlights. I squeeze shut my brakes and run to you. Thanks to God it is I who find you so late at night.'

She had a sudden clear flash of remembrance, of him helping her tenderly into his taxi, the warm fusty man's smell inside, of tobacco and stuffiness, the car radio still playing, like a bubble of light in the wet shining dark.

She smiled at him.

'You were my guardian angel to save me like that.'

'*Elle était un peu folle,*' he mouthed severely to Mara over Grace's head as if she were a child. 'So, my angel, you have pink in your cheeks again, eh? You will be back at your Paradiso soon?' He squeezed her hand emotionally. 'I think to myself that the boy from Nouvelle Zélande, that brown girl Porora, even your own *maman* here put too much pressure. They are all too hard on you. These people forget that you are delicate, young, you are still only growing.'

'Delicate,' said Mara, 'is not a word I'd use to describe Grace.'

Raoul frowned at her slightly but Grace could tell he was reluctant to have words with her out of deference to the sickbed atmosphere.

'It could be very dangerous for you. They broke all the woods for the outside of the motel that night. They say thousands of dollars to pay for the motel damage. The motel are saying it is the meeting held by the Communists that started all this. Your boyfriend,' he said to Grace seriously.

'It does sound suspiciously like an act of love,' Mara said.

'It wasn't him,' Grace said shakily, closing her eyes. 'You've got it wrong again, Mara.'

'People are talking, of course. They are no fools, those bastards. They are very happy at the damages but they say nothing to me. They have no witnesses, I hear. So there is nothing to prove for them. You follow me?' Grace opened one eye to look at his face, but he was gazing so tenderly down at her that she closed it again, reassured.

'*Tapu*, they call it. *Tapu*,' he said.

There was a silence in the room.

'I also saw your boyfriend. Jack. He was in the bar. He say to me, please tell Grace I'm thinking of coming back. He say if she want me.'

Grace lay there, her eyes squeezed shut, she felt the pleasure and pain of it in the very base of her spine. She couldn't stop smiling.

'How touching,' her mother said. 'Such passionate naked will. Was he too scared to come himself?'

'No, he just doesn't want to take unfair advantage,' she said as calmly as she could. 'He's as kind as Raoul.' It was a declaration to make to Mara.

'Of course he is kind. He loves you. *Entendu.* You are so young.' Raoul smiled reminiscently, 'Jack was a very drunk man. He have tears in his eyes when he talks of you.'

'It's no life,' said Mara smoking again. 'No life for me.'

Outside their window the scent from the frangipani tree and the morning heat rose together in clouds and Grace could see the rain from last night glistening on the glossy leaves. The sky was turning a brassy blue, already it was beating up into a sultry day.

FOURTEEN

Afterwards at nightfall she went for a walk. It was about the time that Jack's plane was to take off and she had her goodbyes to make. She wanted to see the lights of the plane in the sky, imagine him sitting there in his unfamiliar city clothes, drinking and gazing out the window down into the darkness.

On the road she stood with her head tipped back to watch for him. The night was warm and clinging and full of secrets, the scent of night flowers washed over her like rain. She could hear the laughter of people fishing way out at sea. A strange trick of sound made their voices carry as if they were standing just behind her whispering tenderly in her ear.

At that silent hour when everyone else in the town was sleeping, the whining saws, bulldozers, the traffic of the daytime were blotted out as if they had never existed. The jungle crowded right up onto the road, it was heavy with secret life, the presence of long-forgotten people and vanished worlds, spirits stealing back from the past. As she started to walk again she was dissolved in the softness and infinity of the Pacific. The jungle, the endless murmuring plain of dark sea, the depths of the tropical night sky seemed to go on forever and merge into one patient immensity.

She watched the sky for a while longer before turning disappointed for home, walking so quietly along their overgrown path that even the lizards sleeping on the stones did not move. The house lay shadowed by the jungle and the mountain, its friendly bulk looming up suddenly in front of her.

As she came up onto the verandah she saw without surprise that her mother was sitting there, smoking, waiting for her.

'There she goes,' she said as the lights of the plane burst upwards in a shower of stars in the distance. They both watched it in silence.

'Don't think I don't know how you feel,' Mara said when the sky was quiet again. 'And don't think ever that I don't know what kind of person you are. There'll always be others, even if you don't believe it now. A girl like you is a miracle to the world.'

They sat looking out onto the dark vines of their tangled garden. For no particular reason Grace thought of a painting she'd seen in a school library book years ago by a Russian, of an angel playing his fiddle in the blue air, soaring over the trees in a glorious dreamlike world. At the time it had reminded her of her mother's stories.

Sitting out on the verandah in the safe dark she remembered the angel's serene face and realised that she was closer to understanding it than she had ever thought. She had already discovered that there were mysterious forces moving in the world — angels, spirits, devils — and that there was a whole shimmering edifice of lies and wonder to explore before she was fully grown.